The Last Husband
and Other Stories

The Last Husband
and Other Stories

by

WILLIAM HUMPHREY

Short Story Index Reprint Series

BOOKS FOR LIBRARIES PRESS
FREEPORT, NEW YORK

Grateful acknowledgment is made to the following period-icals for permission to reprint stories which appeared origi-nally in their pages:

The New Yorker, for "Quail for Mr. Forester"

The Sewanee Review, for "The Hardys" and "The Fauve"

Accent, for "In Sickness and Health" and "Man with a Family"

Harper's Bazaar, for "Sister"

The Quarterly Review of Literature, for "A Fresh Snow"

INTERNATIONAL STANDARD BOOK NUMBER:
0-8369-3675-2

LIBRARY OF CONGRESS CATALOG CARD NUMBER:
75-132118

PRINTED IN THE UNITED STATES OF AMERICA

Contents

~~~~~~

The Last Husband
and Other Stories

The Last Husband

~~~~~~

I

Our honeymoon was over one bright warm Monday in late November when Janice drove me down to catch the 8:02 and I became a commuter.

There was a fine invigorating pinch in the air and standing on the station platform with my new wife and new brief case and my unpunched commutation ticket, I was conscious of looking like a young man of whom a lot was expected and who expected a lot of himself, and I did not care who saw. I did not need to care, I soon began to feel, for no one noticed me.

They did notice when Janice kissed me good-by. I was the only man whose wife kissed him, and I waited with Janice to be the last on the train. Then I saw why no other man got a kiss—nearly all their women got on the train with them; they were going to work, too. Janice was almost the only person left on the platform as the train pulled out.

Needless to say, while honeymooning we had been content not to know anyone in Cressett. But now we were eager to meet people. It was not by chance that we had come to make our home among them, for while not everyone in Cressett was an advertising artist like me, enough of them did things similar to give the place a name. But though people in the streets had smiled and some had said hello, they smiled more as if they were afraid they knew you and said hello as if they feared perhaps they ought to know you. I'd had to admit to myself that I'd not seen a really friendly face, and after walking down the aisle of the train that morning, down that double row of grumpy, unrested faces—the few, that is, that were visible, for most of them were protected by newspapers—my hopes of seeing one were at their lowest.

Then I encountered the smile of Edward Gavin. He was sitting by the window beneath which Janice stood to wave to me. He was not the only man my age, but he was the only one who looked as if he felt himself to be. It was when I asked if I might share his seat that he gave me his smile. Such politeness as mine, or perhaps it was my desire to share a seat with anyone, apparently confirmed my innocence, for several people turned and smiled. But my man's smile was a friendly smile.

He nodded toward Janice and asked, "Married long?"

"Two months," I said.

He spared me the pleasantries. In fact, after telling me his name he said nothing. I told about myself, pausing often to let him say something, but he didn't, and finally, growing ashamed of my egotism, I said, "Married yourself?"

"Twenty years," he said wearily.

I smiled. But I was at that stage of my own when to hear a man joke about his marriage was not funny to me. "It doesn't seem to have hurt you," I could not help saying.

To my surprise he got to his feet. The train was slowing for Webster's Bridge, the first stop after Cressett. That was where this man Edward Gavin got off, having commuted just three miles.

Being the last stop on the line, barely within commuting distance, Cressett was the starting point for the morning train, the 8:02. The coach was empty when we came in and each man and woman took a seat to himself, like a herd of milch cows trained to go to their separate stalls. Oh, I noticed pairs who sat together daily, but I noticed also that after a grunt or two they settled down to as deep a silence as those who sat alone until their seats were shared by strangers getting on at stops down the line; indeed, I decided that those pairs had agreed to sit together just to keep each from having to sit with anyone he disliked even more. And so for me the coach came soon to have the atmosphere of an elevator ride prolonged for nearly two hours. The evening train, which had a lounge car and which set out from Grand Central loaded full of people going home from work, promised to be more sociable. But I learned quickly that if anything can make a person more ill-tempered than having to go to work in the morning, it's having to go home in the evening, and so the occasional gusts of sociability from the gin rummy games on the evening train only intensified the general incivility.

I found myself thinking again of the man Gavin's smile. I looked out for him and saw that he sat regularly with no one but that he did not seem to resent it quite so much as others if someone sat with him. He lived in Webster's Bridge, I knew now, having seen him board the train there every morning since the first, so when we stopped there one morning, the seat next to me being empty, of course, I invited him with a look to take it. He

11

seemed to recognize me with something other than pleasure; in response to my look he frowned deeply, and he took a seat up the aisle.

Coming home that night, as we drew up the line, I left my seat and worked my way up to the head coach. Edward Gavin was there. The sight of him then was something of a shock. Slumped in his seat, abandoned to his exhaustion, he resembled nothing so much as an elder brother of the man I had seen before. But when he saw me he drew himself together and his smile performed the most amazing transformation on his face, as when a photographic print lies in the developer and the washed-out features of a face suddenly collect themselves into life. I forgave him completely his unfriendliness of the morning. Tell yourself there's nothing personal in it, that anyone else could do just as much—still it does something to you, makes you feel good, to have your approach bring that much change to a person's face.

I said, however, that if he did not feel like talking to anyone . . .

He rejected vigorously the implication that he was tired, commanded me to sit, and talked with animation. Then the conductor came in and announced Webster's Bridge. I gathered up my topcoat and brief case and stood in the aisle to let him out.

He made no move.

"This is only Webster's Bridge," he said.

I was about to reply when I saw that his eyes had narrowed strangely, narrowed with something very much like suspicion. Then I saw that upon his lips had come a playful, almost sinister smile. He seemed to be daring me to ask for an explanation.

"Oh," I said. "Oh, yes," and sat down.

My bewilderment quickly gave way to fear. He seemed to know this and to be enjoying it. We rode silently for what seemed a long while. When he finally offered to talk it was not to ease me. For the time left he chatted gaily and forced me to answer his questions, and all the while he kept smiling his playful, sinister smile.

When he boarded the train next morning at Cressett he did not share my seat because I'd made sure he couldn't by sharing someone else's and because I was hiding behind a newspaper. But I distinctly felt that he knew I was behind that paper; I could feel his smile coming right through it. Nor did I ride out with him that evening. Again, sitting behind my paper, I felt he knew I was in the same coach; in fact, though I had waited until I saw him seated and then gone to another coach, he had come into my coach when we were a few miles up the line. And his knowing I was there did nothing to keep him from getting off—and with an air as careless, as regular as you please—at Webster's Bridge—*only* Webster's Bridge!

I watched him for a week. One morning he would get on one place, the next morning the other. One night he would get off at Webster's Bridge, then take the train at Cressett the next morning, and another time it would be the other way around. Sometimes he'd take the train at neither place, yet be in Grand Central and take the train out that evening.

I would often look around me to find if any of the others noticed these goings-on, or to find if any observed my interest. Everyone was busy or tired from a busy day, everyone was too self-absorbed, and I felt silently reprimanded for my idle nosiness—which did nothing to check it, as you may imagine. I may say, though, that after a few looks around at my tired and busy and self-absorbed fellow passengers, I was ready to give Edward Gavin my sympathy if his only reason was to have a little variety in his life and be different from them, who got on and off at the same stop every day.

After three weeks something happened, but for which I suppose I should have lost interest and should have forced myself to find some perfectly logical and prosaic explanation for him, and have forgotten the man altogether, especially if I could have found someone who looked at all pleasant to ride with. It was this:

One night the person sitting in front of me got off at the stop before Webster's Bridge, revealing Gavin sitting in the head of the coach. I fell to thinking of him and his two train stops and I became so absorbed in it, said the names of the two towns to myself so many times, that when the conductor came in and announced Webster's Bridge I got up, put on my coat, took up my things and got off the train.

As I was walking down the platform still puzzling and looking for Janice in the crowd, I realized my mistake and felt so foolish that instead of chasing after the train as it pulled out I stood stock-still. When I did begin to run it was too late and at the end of the platform I gave up and stood panting for breath. Then I saw a man standing in the red platform lights, his hand on the door of a station wagon inside which sat a woman. It was Gavin, and he was staring at me wildly.

The next afternoon as I hurried up the platform in Grand Central I found myself overtaken by him. He smiled as though nothing had happened, asked if I was riding with anyone, whether I had got into a rummy

14

foursome yet, and when I finally managed to say "no," suggested that we ride up together. "After all," he said in a side-of-the-mouth way as he gave me a hand up the steps, "we'd might as well be as friendly as possible under the circumstances, hadn't we?"

We were barely seated when he said, "Strange, isn't it, what jealousy can do to a person? Read a story the other day about an old couple who'd been married fifty years and all that time the woman had lived in jealousy of the husband's dead first wife. Now, the author takes you inside the husband's mind early in the story and you know that he had completely forgotten that first wife. You see the irony. Woman might have had a full life. There it was just waiting for her. If it hadn't been for her jealousy. For which she had no reason at all. Isn't that just like people? Women especially. Take my wife now—"

I must have blushed at this sudden, tasteless confidence.

"You know my wife," he said, and it was not a question.

"Not at all," I hastily replied.

He smiled at me knowingly, intimately. "Come now," he said. "You an advertising artist and new in town and don't know my wife?" His tone was quite insultingly incredulous. Apparently those two qualifications of mine were enough to make his wife certain to know me. He then gave me another long, sly, familiar smile, which, to my amazement, I saw was meant to convince me that there was no use trying to deny that I knew his wife.

"Alice, you know, has this one fixed idea," he said. "The same as the woman in that story. Comes from sitting home all day with nothing to do, so her imagination gets somewhat—hmm—" he leered—"inflamed."

Imagine telling this to a stranger!

"Poor Alice," he said, and he shook his head sadly. "Of

15

course, I guess I *haven't* been always as model a husband
as the one in that story," he added slyly. "*Poor* Alice," he
insisted. "No-o, no, I guess you couldn't say I've always
been *that* model," and in the tone of this was considerably
less of genuine repentance than of fond reminiscence. Then
he seemed to have caught himself saying too much. "It's
got so bad, Alice's jealousy, I mean, that I can't even keep
a secretary. I have to keep one on the sly in Webster's
Bridge and work with her in the evenings. I don't have to
tell you what Alice thinks I'm out doing those evenings.
You may wonder why I risk keeping her just three miles
down the line from home. But doesn't that prove how
innocent"—he laid a broad emphasis on the word, and
as though that weren't enough, accompanied it with a
wink—"it all is? Would I be so stupid if it was something
more?" He had thought this out carefully and was obviously pleased with it. He wanted to avert my suspicions,
but at the same time he was obviously too proud of his
prowess to resist letting me in on the truth, so that it all
added up to the most proudly guilty protestation of innocence you ever saw.

Well, it was all so strange that I did not immediately
realize its implication for me. Then the night when he
had said that this was only Webster's Bridge came back
to me, and his wild glare beneath the station lamp the
night before, and I realized that he thought I had deliberately watched and followed him. I was insulted and
about to tell him so, and then I had to ask myself what
else could the man think on seeing me, breathless from
running, on the platform of the station where he knew I
did not belong, where I had tried to lure him into getting
off before. No wonder he was sure I knew his wife. He

16

probably thought, and well he might from the look of things, that I was in her pay.

I said, "Mr. Gavin, if you've got troubles with your wife, I—well, I'm very sorry." My stupidity infuriated me. "But, but I assure you—" and here I got infuriated at my pompousness—"that I do not know your wife. I don't even know you! Last night—well, last night I, I got off the train at the wrong stop, that is at Webster's Bridge, out of pure absentmindedness. Pure absentmindedness. And when I realized my mistake I ran after the train and I missed it, as you know." I could have kicked myself for that "as you know." I was conscious also that people were turning to stare, for I had grown a bit loud. Now I whispered, "If you think I had any other reason, why, then, why you're wrong, that's all. And, really, you ought to look into things a little further before you come up to a man and begin accusing— well, forget it!" And with this I left him and found a seat in another coach, cured of my loneliness for a train companion.

II

Imagine my astonishment when after this the man seemed to go out of his way to bump into me on the train, in the stations and on the street in Cressett. I chose a different coach each morning and evening but he always found me and on the evening train if the seat beside me was taken he took the nearest seat and waited until the person beside me got off. He made no mention of what had passed between us, but he seemed to feel it had given us the basis for a close friendship, close enough for him to wink at me now when he got off the train in the evening at Webster's Bridge and to show me with a leer what an exhausting night he had had of it when he got on in the morning. He boasted so much I began to have suspicions.

He was pretty crude, and so I was not eager to accept his offer to drive me home from the station one night. Janice had phoned in the afternoon to say that our car was in the garage. Gavin saw me getting into the taxi and hurried over and was so insistent that I had to give in.

On the way he slowed at a side road and suggested stopping in at his place for a drink. I did not protest. I wanted to get a look at his wife.

"Like you to meet my wife," he said grimly.

Beneath the name Gavin on his mailbox was the name Metsys.

"Any relation to—"

"Sister."

I was thinking, as you have no doubt guessed, of Victoria Metsys, the woman who, by drawing upon Picasso, Klee and Miro for her subway posters, had started a whole new trend in advertising art twenty years ago. Gavin seemed nonchalant enough, I thought, about having her in the family. This I could understand better when I saw his house: he had not done badly himself.

A man bringing you to meet his wife could not very well prepare you by saying, "Oh, by the way, you must expect her to look twenty years older than I." But if Gavin had, he would have saved an awkward moment when I said to myself, "Why, she must be fifty!" and what I was thinking showed all too plainly on my face. This must have been painful enough for Mrs. Gavin, but the next moment I made things worse by turning involuntarily, as though I needed to recheck his age, for another look at Edward. What I saw in his face then explained why he had not prepared me; it was not the first time he had enjoyed this trick.

We sat, and while Gavin told her about me I studied his face. I could believe now that he was her age, but the way he had chosen to show me was the only way I could have been convinced of it. It was the way his face was made that gave it its youthful look. It was thin and small, there would never be much flesh on it to sag, and the overall impression it gave was one of such boyish fun that the lines around his eyes and the corners of his mouth would for a long while yet be thought to come from laughter rather than from years.

Gavin left the room to mix drinks and the first thing Alice said to me was, "I'm older than my husband, you know." It took coolness to come out with it like that. I had wondered already how she met this problem—it was too big for silence—and I admired her way. Then, "Two years," she said, and though I didn't doubt her, this specification somehow robbed the thing of its daring self-assurance.

I said, "You're Victoria Metsys' sister, aren't you?"

It had not occurred to me that she might be something in her own right and that *Alice* Metsys was a name I ought to know, or pretend I knew, as well as Victoria. Her smile showed me my mistake. It was a smile that had had a lifetime of service in answer to that remark, "Oh, *Victoria's* sister!"

She knew my work, it seemed, and talking about it served as the excuse for showing me some of hers, hers of a certain period, she said, which mine reminded her of —not, she added, that she meant to accuse me of copying her. She thumbed through some magazines kept under the end table, though they were, at the newest, five years old and two of them defunct, and found some "little spot fillers she had tossed off, just to help out the editors," and a four-inch ad for a short-lived breakfast food which I'd forgotten all about but now remembered trying once and then a year later, when I was packing to move, discovering the box on the shelf alive with weevils. Her work bore no resemblance whatever to mine. What it was like, embarrassingly like, was the highly individual work with which her sister Victoria had burst upon the world twenty years ago. She might not enjoy being Victoria's sister, I thought, but if she hadn't been, those drawings would never have been published.

Gavin reminded me of the time and said he didn't want my wife mad at him for holding up dinner. But Alice said she had to show me the house. She seemed, in fact, to feel she had to show and tell me everything about herself in the few minutes before I went home.

I praised every room we passed through on our way to the conservatory, and I praised that, though not quite strongly enough, it seemed. She was wild about flowers herself, she said, and I could believe it, for in this room it was as if the spring and summer had been brought in out of the cold. So I waxed appreciative and said of a peony that I had never seen such a lovely chrysanthemum. She seemed to have extravagantly high hopes for our similarities and sympathies, and this disappointed her unreasonably. But it appeared that one way or the other she was not going to permit the least difference between us, for she then said in a confidential tone, "To tell you the truth, I don't really care a lot for flowers myself."

What she did care about was setting me right on one point without delay. She was afraid I thought something was being put over on her, and she wanted me to save my pity.

"You might think I don't know what's going on, living back here in this wilderness—immured, as you might say. But I manage to know pretty well, considering that I never learned to drive a car. Edward, you know, always discouraged me from learning. And I used to think it was because he enjoyed having me dependent on him. Well, I just want you to know that I know all about Edward."

"All about—"

"All about his philanderings, of course," she said impatiently. "Don't pretend you don't know about them. Everybody knows about Edward's philanderings. Poor boy, he thinks he is so careful and so clever and he gives himself away every time he turns around."

I remembered our encounter in the train and I could not help laughing.

"Yes, it is amusing, isn't it?" she said. "And at the same time rather touching. I think that's why I like him, you know—he is such a poor liar. He's always working up some little affair for himself and he can hardly enjoy it for fear I'm going to find out. In fact, I sometimes believe that his real pleasure is in thinking he's putting something over on me, and not in the poor girl herself at all. Just now it's some little beauty parlor operator down in the city."

I supposed she had not been as recently posted as she thought. Then I decided that she simply hadn't bothered to keep up to date.

"I can't tell Edward this, you understand. It would hurt his pride. He'd hate to know I had known all along despite his elaborate pains, and he would die to know I didn't mind. I just didn't want you to think I was a perfect fool. So," she concluded in an intimate tone, as though we were

21

both long accustomed to pampering him, "don't let on to him that I know. Let him have his fun."

Naturally, her anxiety to set me right so quickly made me suspicious. It hardly seemed likely that she could care so little, that her vanity should not have been at least a little wounded by her husband's escapades. But by the time I left I was pretty well convinced that none of her vanity was invested in her husband. As soon as she got over this one hurdle she could think of nothing—certainly not of how late she was keeping me—except her "work," and I gathered that it left her no time to care what Edward did with himself. Moreover, I got the feeling about her that she was just as happy to have Edward busy himself in that way elsewhere.

III

All afternoon I watched the snow swirl past my office window and at three I phoned Janice to ask how much had fallen in Cressett. I was thirty minutes getting a line through and I learned that there it was worse than in the city, that it had given way now to a steady rain that was turning everything to ice.

In Grand Central it was announced that frozen switches would hold the schedule up all night. A single train might get through around 1:00 A.M. I decided to stay over in town. I was turning away with the rest of the crowd by the gate when my arm was caught.

"Staying over?" asked Gavin. "Ah. Haven't had your dinner, I don't suppose. Since we're stranded down here why don't we make the worst of it together?"

I said I would have to call Janice and Gavin stood with me in the long line of conscientious husbands waiting for the telephone booths and when my turn came I said, "Like me to tell my wife to call yours and tell her?"

"Don't bother," he said. "She wouldn't believe it."

Out in the street the snow had stopped and it was hard to believe that it was not possible to get home to Janice tonight. We decided on a hotel and registered for rooms and then Gavin knew a restaurant on Forty-first Street. They knew him, too, for the waiter said, "I thought you might be turning up here tonight, Mr. Gavin."

We ordered drinks.

"Well, here's how," said Gavin. But he stopped his glass at his lips, a shrewd smile formed on them and his eyes went hard. I looked at him questioningly, as he seemed to be waiting for me to do. "Hmmm," he said. "The waiter wasn't the only one who thought I might be turning up here tonight."

He left this quivering on the air, then, "See that man over there—don't look now."

I waited a decent interval, then bent to pick up my napkin and stole a glance at the little bald man at the bar. "Don't tell me he's anyone worth knowing," I said.

Gavin gave me his smile of mystery and left me to wait.

"No-o," he mused, looking up suddenly from his drink, "just a private eye."

I was touched, and so I used a gentle tone in saying, "Well now, I believe you once thought I might be a detective hired by your wife, too."

This did not have the effect I had intended. "Yes!" he cried, much amused. "Things were going very badly just then, and I must have been seeing detectives everywhere I looked." Then he nodded towards the bar and said, "He knows I've spotted him, so he'll pay his check and leave in a minute. Poor guy. What a job. And on a night like this."

"Then how do you know that man is a detective any more than I was?" I asked.

"Oh, I can tell," he said earnestly. "I really wasn't very sure about you, you know."

"Oh," I said, "not very sure. Just sure enough to—"

"Look," he said. "See? He's paid his check and left, just as I told you."

"Yes," I said. "I suppose that's proof enough."

He nodded.

"Let me tell you something," I said.

"I'll bet I can tell you what you're going to say," he said. "You're going to tell me I have nothing to worry about from my wife."

He must have seen from my face that he had hit it right. He went on, "I'm sure that's what she gave you to feel the other night when you had your little tête-à-tête. I suppose she told you something like this: 'Poor Edward. Really, it's pathetic. He's just like a little boy who thinks he's putting something over on his mother.'"

He mimicked her with amazing accuracy, and looking at that boyish face of his it was hard to keep in mind that he had lived with her voice for twenty years.

"Don't you see," he continued, "it's proof she needs. Whenever she meets a new person she tries to get some by pretending she doesn't care about the whole thing."

Well, this was possible, of course, and for a moment I wavered. Then I recalled his wife's obsession with her career. I said, "Don't you see that your wife is too interested in her so-called work to care—"

"Hah! Her so-called work!" He laughed so loudly that the couple in the booth across the floor turned to stare.

24

"And you ought to know!" he cried. "I've always said so, of course, but you're a real professional. Pathetic stuff, isn't it? But tell me," he leaned across the table and whispered, "you didn't give anything away, did you? You didn't mention Webster's Bridge, I hope. It's very handy for me having things set up like that. And besides its being so convenient, I can't help being just a little proud of it. The last place she thinks to look is right under her nose. The very nearest town. In fact, right over the mountain behind her house! You didn't, did you?"

"I didn't! What do you think—"

"Of course," he said, "it wouldn't have made the least difference if you had."

This was exactly what I myself had been going to say. It was disconcerting, this way he had of lifting phrases out of my mind and putting them to his use.

"Because she has such pride," he said, "that if you told her it had been right under her nose all along then she *couldn't* let herself believe it. I wish you had told her. I ought to draw her a map to the place and tell her the best hours to find me there. Then she could never let herself believe it. Next time she asks you, tell her!"

"Let me tell you an easier way to put an end to your fears," I said. "You don't have anything to—"

Suddenly he looked weary and apologetic and he gave a sigh. "Charley, forgive me," he said. "Forget it all. I'm sorry to have dragged you into this mess. Why, we're almost strangers. I appreciate it, don't think I don't. But don't let yourself get involved. Don't let me talk to you about it. It's been going on like this for years and—here. Here's the waiter. Eat your dinner and forget it."

After dinner he suggested a show. We strolled over towards Broadway. We stopped to shelter a light for cigarettes. We moved on and Gavin jerked a thumb over his shoulder. "To think," he said, "it's my money that guy's getting for trailing me."

"Why, that's not even the same man!" I cried. "Are you blind as well?"

"Of course it's not the same man." Gavin was being patient with me. "The first one knew I'd spotted him, so this one relieved him. They always work in pairs."

"Look," I said, pointing to where the man stood innocently examining the billboard of a musical revue. "He's just somebody out looking for something to do with himself. Listen, you'd better get a grip on yourself. You'd better—"

"Well, so long as I'm paying for it," he said grimly, "I might as well have fun."

He edged up close to this pudgy little man and stressing his words for his benefit, said, "Hell, Charley, do you mean to tell me that the best you can do on a night away from the wife is a girlie show? Now come with me and I'll show you a real hot time. (See him take that down in his notebook?)"

"That's his wallet and he's counting his money!" I whispered.

It was one of those standing sandwich boards with pictures of the chorus girls and this tired little man had moved around to the other side for a look at the rest of them. He was rubbing his hands because of the cold and this gesture gave him the look of an old-fashioned lecher, an impression of which he was aware. His timid excitement shone on his face and I took him for a salesman in town for the night, whose main enjoyment of this show would come from thinking all through it of his unsuspecting wife sitting at home in Weehawken or somewhere. He had heard what Gavin said—he could not have helped hearing—and he leered at me around the sandwich board to let me know that he, too, was out on a spree.

Meanwhile Gavin was rattling on. "Listen, Charley, this is kid stuff." (This, too, the little drummer or whatever he was heard, and frowned; Gavin was belittling the fun he had planned for himself.) "I'll get us a couple of hot numbers to warm this winter evening. How do you like yours, married or single? I like mine already broken in. I once knew a little woman in White Plains. Her husband was a salesman, always out on the road, and that made things very nice. He's probably caught out on the road somewhere tonight. She was all right, let me tell you. Those salesmen's wives, they don't get much and they're always ready for—"

Now the little man flung a look at Gavin and strode away from the marquee in dignified outrage.

"Listen, Charley," he said, projecting his voice after the retreating figure, "let's rent a car and go up to Webster's Bridge. I'll phone my girl and tell her to get in a friend for you!"

"Ssh!" I hissed. "If the man *was* a detective—" Was I going as crazy as he?

"Well, that'll give her something to think about," he said, standing with his hands on his hips and watching his detective slip off to make his report.

I would try one last time to disabuse him. "Now, Gavin," I began, patiently, sympathetically, "believe me. You have nothing to fear from your wife. Nothing. She doesn't care what you do with yourself so long as—"

He was beginning to smile tolerantly at me again.

"Listen. Do you know what she said to me? 'Let him have his fun,' she said."

27

"Now, Charley," he said, "think a minute. Does that sound likely to you?"

IV

Gavin did not feel it was disloyal of me to go to Alice's teas. He assumed that I shared his judgment of Alice and her circle and he thought my duplicity a good joke on her. In the beginning I went often. Gavin was never there; he hated the men who came even more than the women; and that desperate and phantom fear he had of Alice became all the more pathetic when I observed that I never once heard her mention his name.

Perhaps Gavin's judgment did influence me, for from the start I felt myself obscurely unsuited to that crowd. This seemed unnatural, for they were the people with whom I ought to have felt most in sympathy, so I kept going there in an effort to overcome it, or at least to determine whose fault it was, theirs or mine. And finally I went back because Alice was so importunate.

Alice was always eager to ingratiate herself with a new person; she was especially so with me. Perhaps because I had met Edward first she felt she had to work to overcome a certain prejudice in me. When she learned, as she somehow learned all her sister's movements, that I had met Victoria, she had, she thought, and she was not far wrong, another prejudice to overcome in me. She was even more anxious for my company when during the winter it became known that I'd landed a fair-sized contract.

The price of admission to one of Alice's teas was a slow, worried shake of the head in answer to her question, "How is your work going?"

Now Alice had the best ear in Cressett for whisperings

that some person was on his way up, or on his way out, and it was only because your work was known to be going very well that you had been asked to her house. But . . .

"Oh, that's too bad," she would say sympathetically, and the more successful you were known to be the more her face beamed with satisfaction. "But then, what do you expect?" she would say. "If you keep on doing the same old things year after year they love you, but just try something a bit new and they're afraid to risk it." This was directed at her sister Victoria, who was doing very well indeed on the same old thing. Alice herself was forever changing her "style" abruptly and trying something new, "experimenting" as she called it. Her final words of consolation would be, "Well, we all seem to be in a slump just now, but we'll come out of it, won't we?"

Her having chosen me as the special object of her attentions had the effect of making Alice all the more uneasy with me. Her fear of failing to impress me made her urgent and shrill. She always had a look of being too concerned with what she was going to say when I was done talking to pay any attention to me. This made conversation with her rather a sequence of non sequiturs. On top of this, when she did begin to talk she forgot what she had been so carefully planning to say, and chattered desperately, frowning with anxiety over my opinion of her. If I had not observed all these things on first meeting her it was because, unlike most people, who grow more relaxed with you with time, Alice was at her best in the first five minutes of your acquaintance.

She was worried about the invitation, she said, the way she had worded it, afraid she had written asking me please *not* to come to tea Friday at five, and would not let me assure her that she had made no such mistake, but kept me ten minutes at the door while she told of the many embarrassments this habit of hers of being positive when she meant to be negative and vice versa had got her into, how she once lost a dear friend through the constraint between them after she had written and then not been sure whether she said she was glad to hear that she was now home from the hospital, or glad she was not home.

By the time she came to the end of her speech she was frowning with irritation, for she always feared that in her urge to be intimate she might have let something slip that showed her unfavorably. But mostly she was annoyed with the time it took her. Words did take time, and—strange as it may seem in a person who rarely stopped—Alice hated to talk. One ought to appreciate her nature, she felt, without her having to explain it to him, through silent, sympathetic feeling.

When at last she let me join the guests I saw at once the reason for her unusual discomfiture. Her sister had come—uninvited, I was sure, just as I was sure that Victoria's sole reason for coming would be to make Alice uncomfortable.

My acquaintance with Victoria had begun when I turned to find her standing behind me in the Cressett gallery one day, asking me please to tell her why I had avoided her. She was not used to being snubbed for three months by new young artists in town, she said, and when I tried to say something she stopped me with, "Why not say right out that my little sister has told you what a witch I am? Then I can prove what a false notion you've been given." When she left me I realized that she had not felt it necessary to tell me who she was.

Now Alice left her station by the door and joined us

and did just what I had told myself she would if she ever got her sister to one of her parties. To be known as Victoria's sister had been the burden of her life, and yet in front of others she was willing to take the credit they gave it. So now she was exhibiting her to her guests and loudly praising her latest work, a series of billboards that had been plastered all over the nation and which among us artists had caused a lot of talk. And joining in with Alice's praises was Robert, Victoria's husband.

Even in writing it, it is hard not to call Robert Mr. Metsys. But already this afternoon Victoria had loudly let a new person know that her name was Mrs. Hines. It amused me that she, who had made the name Metsys famous, was superior to it, while Alice, who had suffered from being the sister of the woman who had made it famous, and who had certainly not done much to enlarge its fame, clung to it to the point that she signed checks and invitations and laundry lists with it. But if it amused me, it amused Victoria much more. She also enjoyed belittling poor Robert by using his undistinguished name. A subtle pleasure, but Victoria's pleasures were.

Now she had taken all she could of Robert's and Alice's praises. "*Kitsch!*" she said. "That's the word for what I do. At least *I*," she looked pointedly around at the members of her audience, "know it."

Alice smiled to her guests to indicate that this was Victoria's modesty. I had once made the same mistake. Now Victoria's eyes flashed as they had flashed at me. She had no more mock modesty than she had genuine modesty. She was genuinely irate. She wanted everyone to know that she was superior to the way in which she made her money.

She spoke of the men from whom she had stolen, of Picasso and Klee and Miro, and of her guilt for what she had done to them—"What I have done to them in the process of converting them into this," she had said to me my first night at her place, waving her hand around her sumptuous drawing room, and I had remarked to myself that nothing could have better shown how very expensive the room had been. It was an unexpected attitude and gave her, if I may so express it, a marvelous extension of personality. In fact, before that evening was over she had made it seem almost purer in spirit to have done what she had and *know* it, than to have refused to do it, and I had felt myself beginning to appreciate the moral pleasure she took in this role.

Now one of her listeners made the second of the mistakes I had made that night, and said that he, too, could probably, if he searched himself for a moment, find a few such thefts on his conscience, whereupon in the look she gave him she revealed her belief that nobody had a conscience but her. Then she turned to abuse her husband with the gusto with which I had seen her do it.

"*Kitsch!*" she flung at him. "Bad enough to dirty your own good ideas, but to steal and pervert the ideas of others —and when those others are the big men of the age!"

Oh, she was at least a big thief. We others stole from her; she stole from the source itself.

"*Kitsch!*" she flung at him one last time. Poor man, she had left him nothing but his wife, and she would not let him have even a belief in her.

I remembered the first time I saw him. We had left our car at the foot of the steep snow-covered drive, Janice and I. We had not walked far when up at the house a dog barked, and then piano music had started up and floated down to us on the still winter air. It accompanied us all the way, a passage from *The Well-tempered Clavichord*, terribly difficult and very well done. After knocking at the door we had had to wait through half a dozen measures for the end. Then Robert, whom I actually did call Mr. Metsys and he did not correct me, greeted us in sneakers, faded corduroys and a tattered denim jumper, which, as he was well aware, made a striking contrast to the splendor behind him as he stood in the door.

I pointed to the piano and said, "Please go on."

"He can't."

It was Victoria who had come gliding into the room unheard. "He can't go on, that's all he knows."

Robert had smiled modestly, as though that was her way of bragging about him. As a matter of fact, it was true. Those thirty-odd measures of Bach were literally all the music he knew. Every time we went there the same passage began when our arrival at the foot of the hill was announced by the bark of the dog, and at the door each time we had to wait until it was finished in a final burst of triumphant virtuosity.

Robert knew music about as he knew sculpture. There was one promising carving in the hall off the drawing room which he modestly owned to. When I asked to see more I was told by Victoria that there weren't any more, he had done that one and then given up. It was not the first such mistake I'd made in the course of our acquaintance, having asked why he never went on with playwriting or anthropology, so to Victoria it seemed time for a general explanation, though I tried desperately to suggest that I didn't want one. Robert looked penitent while Victoria, in a tolerant scolding tone, a tolerant tone which was the most withering contempt I ever want to hear, explained that Robert's weakness had always been a lack of persistence.

I myself had by this time watched him take up hand printing and fitfully resume the playwriting, and I had seen why he never got anywhere with anything. He was licked before he got a start, Victoria so minimized any effort he made—or, I ought to say, she hardly felt it necessary to minimize them now; his own memory of his past failures was enough to foredoom any new undertaking. Robert still cherished visions of himself succeeding at almost anything, but like those photographer's proofs one takes home to choose among for the final print, they had faded and blurred from being kept too long.

"I'm just lazy," he said.

Yet he worked around the house and grounds ten to twelve hours a day. They pretended their liberal politics as the reason for keeping no hired help, but actually they did not need any. "I'm just lazy"—I supposed he would rather feel he could blame some weakness of his own than admit the true reason for his failures.

I strolled over to talk to Hilda Matthews. Hilda was the woman at whose bidding the country's skirts had once risen an incredible six inches, who had brought back the shingle bob, who had originated the horsetail hairdo. A part of me stood abashed before a woman who could change the look of a whole country like that.

We had talked a while when through the door across the room a new man entered and Hilda said, "Oh, it's my husband. I must go over and say hello."

"Has it been that long since you saw him?"

"I can still recognize him," she said.

"Business, I suppose," I said wisely.

"That's the word we use for it," said Hilda gaily. Whereupon I, who thought I'd been holding up my end of one of those knowing talks about the husband's absences and his excuses, realized how very wrong I had been. It was *she* who had been too busy, or told her husband so, to get home nights. She had assumed I understood it that way.

And perhaps I should have. For the next moment I was joined by John Coefield, who said, "Charley, where's your wife? I haven't seen her in ages."

"Neither have I," I said. "She isn't here."

"Not sick, I hope?"

"No," I confessed, "she's at work."

"Work? Why, I never knew Janice *did* anything."

"She didn't 'do' anything until we came here," I told him. "Now she leaves breakfast for me and takes the early train." I found myself using the half-humorous tone for this which I'd observed in other men, and it irritated me.

Arthur Fergusson, who had come up in time to hear this last, said, "Oh-hoh. Becoming one of us, eh, Charley?"

"No," said John Coefield. "That will be when *he* gets the breakfast and *she* takes the later train."

This had an edge to it, and Arthur Fergusson smiled coldly.

Coefield wore such thick glasses that he seemed to be looking into them rather than through them, but even so he made me understand with a look that he had been trapped once already this afternoon by Arthur. Nothing would ever mean much to Arthur after wartime Washington, his captain's uniform and his desk in the OSS—to say nothing of his African trip. At first, right after the war, while others talked of their experiences, he had made his impression, so I was told, by being silent. Now that that war was a good ways back and people spoke more often of the coming one, he talked incessantly of "his war." He had tried every way in the world to go, had lied unsuccessfully about his age and suffered the humiliation of having a recruiting officer scan his employment record and ask what earthly use he thought he might be to a war effort. But it was one of the things in that record that got him in. He had worked once for an American advertising agency in Morocco, writing copy for soap in three native dialects. So he was sent to recruit natives for spying against the Germans.

Surely he remembered one or two of the many times he had told us about it.

His wife remembered not one or two but all the many times he had told everybody, so she came over soon to extricate us from him.

"You off on Morocco again?" she said, giving us an indulgent shake of the head over Arthur, and giving Arthur a less indulgent look.

Arthur drew himself up and it seemed for a moment he was going to answer back and cause a scene. Then he subsided and gave a sheepish grin.

Coefield said, "Go on, Arthur. You were about to say?"

I thought it was very considerate of Coefield to do that, and quite convincing the look of interest he put on. After a hesitant glance at his wife, Arthur smiled his appreciation.

"You are much too polite, John," said Mary Fergusson.

John Coefield's determined answer surprised me. "Not in the least," he snapped. "Charley and I were absorbed in what Arthur was saying."

Mary shrugged her shoulders and retreated.

A sigh escaped John Coefield as he settled down to Arthur's war again.

We men had gradually drifted together in one corner, and whenever that happened the subject of gardening was bound to come up sooner or later.

One man was a recent convert to organic gardening and he was telling of the dangers to one's health, to the soil, to the national economy, to the very rhythm of nature that came from using chemical fertilizers. They killed earthworms. Now earthworms, he said with much enjoyment of the words, dropped castings that were simply incredibly rich in trace elements, besides keeping the soil aerated by boring holes, networks of holes in it. The great thing about fertilizing with compost was that it was natural. This was admitted by all to be a weighty argument. The word *natural* was a magic word. Moreover, it was felt that the use of artificial fertilizers was not very sporting somehow.

All this made one man who had been prodigal with superphosphate rather uncomfortable. "Well," he demanded, "who had the biggest tomatoes last year, Tom, and the earliest? You or me?"

Bigger, Tom was willing to admit. A day or two earlier perhaps. But as nourishing? What chemical fertilizer did to a tomato was blow it up, force it. But the food value was nil.

Then there was the matter of insecticides. Who wanted to eat arsenic and lead and nicotine with his vegetables?

This man was fifty or so, rather fat, and proud of his callused hands. They showed honest toil and he enjoyed the way they fitted so ill with his job of producing radio programs at fifty thousand dollars a year. I got a vision of him out in his garden before going to the train in the morning raking Mexican beetles into a tin can full of kerosene with a little paddle.

It was growing dusky outside and Alice had turned on no lights but allowed the room to steep in soft grayness. But now it was time for the two groups, the women around one fireplace and the men around the other, to come together for a last exchange before breaking up to go home. To signal the arrival of that moment Alice switched on a lamp.

A change of mood had been coming over me which this sudden light and rustle of activity quickened. The amused, half-contemptuous detachment with which I had been listening to the men now struck me as false and I felt myself filled with a vague dissatisfaction. Suddenly I felt the emptiness of their lives and knew that my own life was no better, no more vigorous. I turned from them.

When I turned I saw Gavin standing in the farthest door, smilingly surveying the room. He had never looked so young, so gay and reckless. From the door he held open came a draft of cool air and to me at that moment he looked like a bringer of fresh air.

Some kind of look was passing between him and the ladies' end of the room. I turned and saw responding to him, unnoticed by all but me, a woman whom I had often seen at Alice's teas. Gavin caught sight of his brother-in-law and pursed his lips with disdain. Then he cast upon the men's corner where I stood a look of utter contempt but reserved a smile for me, and for that I forgave him his insanity. I was glad to be his friend and I recalled with shame the times earlier that I had avoided him.

He strolled over and joined the women. He greeted each one smoothly, concentrating on each that smile of his and all his attention. But when he came to Leila Herschell he blushed, stammered, looked caught, and did a job which a ten-year-old could have bettered in covering up his slip.

Now I knew where I had seen the woman before, in Gavin's station wagon the night I got off the train at Webster's Bridge. I looked at Alice. She was talking with somewhat hysterical unconcern to her brother-in-law. How *she*, Leila, was taking it, I couldn't tell—I never got to know her very well—but it is possible that she was enjoying it.

The thing I couldn't understand was why he had seemed so terribly put out at finding her there, when he had recognized and winked at her from all the way across the room.

By now the men had all gathered round and Gavin went to the portable bar and offered to mix drinks. I think they all sensed the possibility of a scene, for everyone accepted eagerly. He asked each of us—except his brother-in-law, and he pointedly asked Victoria how he wanted his—how each of us took it. But he did not ask Leila Herschell. Hers he mixed automatically. And it was a very personal kind of a drink with a rare combination of ingredients, which Gavin measured and mixed with an all-too-practiced hand. I was spellbound. It took him a long time and in the process he seemed to forget the existence of everyone in the room except her. By this time I was not the only one spellbound. In fact, the only one who was not was Alice, who was trying with desperate chit-chat—the only sound in the room now—to divert the bewitched attention of her neighbors. The last touch was Gavin's tasting the drink himself very deliberately and smacking his lips judiciously, and, satisfied, handing it to Leila with a flourish, all of which seemed to declare an absolute identity of taste between them, developed over a long and intimate period. All this, plus the husky tone in which he spoke to her, was quite enough, but to add one final touch he straightened himself from bending close over her, and, as though sensing the quiet, the stares, suddenly coming to and discovering the enormity of his indiscretion, he hardened his neck and look around at Alice in wide-eyed alarm. It was the best job of bad acting I ever hope to see, and I understood then that was what it was meant to be.

I realized that Gavin had never been trying to conceal his philanderings from Alice, but to make her take notice of them. How I must have wounded him that night when I said she was too wrapped up in her career to care what he did with himself!

I saw him suddenly as a kind of inverted sentimentalist, a believer in marriage—the old-fashioned kind—a man with pride enough left to care if his wife ignored him. He was out of place and out of time, with a pride not to be bent and pacified by the memory of one glamorous, martial, male moment of escape from his routine of meaningless work which any other man could do as well as he and any woman as well as any man, nor in finding something—like gardening—which he could do and his wife couldn't. He took entirely too much pleasure in the mere fact of being unfaithful to his wife, though, who knows, I asked myself, but what in perverse times like ours, perhaps the only way left to honor a thing is in the breach rather than in the observance.

I went home and made my wife promise to give up her job.

V

The next day on the train Gavin and I began playing our game. I was his spy and on mornings after seeing Alice I reported her latest wiles to catch him. He knew it was pure invention and that his "slip" about his mistress had made Alice not a whit more interested, but this called forth our creative abilities and made the game all the more exciting. I quite outdid myself to help him feel hounded and harassed and to feel he was causing her acute distress. Times, I was in some peril of believing it myself.

I pointed out that she was beginning to show wear. She had grown dark circles under her eyes and become careless of her hair and there were days when she looked quite distraught. But the reason, I knew, was the continued failure of her work. She had brought herself at last to come to me for help and this necessity made her almost insulting before she was done. But it was not that which made me so half-hearted in pushing her work. The spectacle of middle-aged love had always appealed to my sentimentality, and though I don't think I quite hoped to bring the Gavins to a state of belated bliss, still I certainly was not going to do anything to help things stay as they were between them, and if Alice were finally discouraged about that career of hers, why, who knew, perhaps she might return to him, become a wife. Stranger things had happened. The Gavins as they were now had happened.

He kept me posted daily, too, on his running skirmish with her, appearing on the train some mornings looking harried and hollow-eyed and hinting darkly how close upon him she was, then the next morning smiling and crafty and pleased with himself at the way he had outfoxed her this time.

He would get off the 6:36 at Webster's Bridge and have dinner with his mistress. Then maybe he would stay, maybe he would go home to Cressett. When he went home he took one of about seven different roads, never allowing himself to decide which until the last moment.

41

He changed cars often, buying each time a different make and color so that none should become familiar to the workers whose houses lay along the back edges of the towns, nor to their children who played in the streets until late at night. After leaving Webster's Bridge all roads climbed above the long valley where in the distance the lights of Cressett lay like scattered coals, and Gavin tried to describe the pleasure it gave him in coming home from his rendezvous to look down on those lights, to glide powerfully through the night past darkened, unsuspecting farmhouses. He felt himself freed from all likeness to the people in those houses, and at the sight of a fox stealing across the road one night with a chicken in its mouth he had felt a thrill of fellowship.

It was clear to me that love was dead between him and Alice. I doubted that there had ever been any. It was not his heart that was wounded by unrequited love, but his pride that was wounded by her ignoring him. I knew it was pride with him, and, if you take my meaning, *male* pride, when he told me that he made a point, even if "Webster's Bridge" (the only name I ever heard him use for his mistress) bored him, of not getting home until after midnight, and that when he came in he made as much noise as possible, for unlike most men, who try to keep their wives from learning how late they've been, Gavin wanted to be sure Alice knew how late he was. There had been times, he told me somewhat shamefacedly, when he had sneaked in so she would not know how early he was.

He was proud of his record of never offering her any excuse for his nights away from home. She was too proud to ask, he said, so she just had to stew in silent fury. He had a variation on this of sometimes offering her an ex-

cuse so transparent it would have insulted the intelligence
of a ten-year-old. Now *that*, I could imagine, *would* irri-
tate Alice.

He told me of evenings he had spent away from home
and not in Webster's Bridge either, but wandering all
night in New York. Once, around five in the morning,
he had found himself near the Battery and he never forgot the sun coming up over East River and the gulls rising
out of the mist. He had stayed away from his mistress
deliberately, so that his torture of Alice would be ab-
stract, pure. I wondered whether, sitting there on the pier
that dawn, he had been able to convince himself that Alice
was lying awake in an agony of jealous suspicion. Or had
he lost by that time all sense of the reason for his act?

He had his own doubts now, and wondered sometimes
if all was right with him in the head. His memory was going bad, for example. Or rather, the worse it got for recent
things, the more vividly he recalled things that had happened to him fifteen and twenty years ago. Things returned
to him in dreams, painful scenes for the most part, in
which he had played a foolish role or done something
despicable. He was depressed often and he assured me
solemnly that he was a much less happy man than I no
doubt imagined. He was always restless and dissatisfied
lately and had even caught himself asking himself such
silly questions as whether he was a success in life. More
and more he found himself, he said with self-contemptu-
ous amazement, *thinking* all the time. He was dissatisfied
with his mistress, for one thing, tired of her; she no longer
excited him. Or rather, he added hastily and with a leer,
other women excited him more. He told me one morning
of having had a woman up at the Cressett house the night
before, having got Alice away on an elaborate pretext (a

simple one would not have satisfied that strong sense of drama which I was beginning to recognize as perhaps his main characteristic) and the delightful thing was that the woman was not his mistress. Oh, she had once been his mistress, but that was long ago, and, as he said, what woman hadn't been his mistress one time or another? He laughed to fill the coach when he thought of not only Alice away on a wild goose chase, but his regular mistress sitting at home in Webster's Bridge, both being deceived at once. There he had had, I said to myself, two wives to be unfaithful to at the same time; was there ever such respect for marriage?

His escapade excited him tremendously, and all the more because he did not understand why. There was something about his enjoyment of such things that mystified him, and more than once he asked me to explain it to him. "Now what makes me do things like that?" he would sober suddenly and say. Yet when I tried to tell him he shut me off at once, just as he always shut off his own self-questionings. He preferred to act on impulse, to be wrong if necessary in what he did, but not to be deliberative. And yet, he said, he had not always been the kind of fellow who, for example, could decide without investigation that I was a detective hired by his wife, and he confessed to just a shade of doubt that the little man in the city that night had been one. But what if he wasn't? What the hell! Deliberation robbed things of excitement. He was too old now, he said, to start looking back over everything he had ever done to find out whether he had been right or wrong.

But, like everyone, he had an urge to understand himself which even he could not always deny. He liked me to ask him questions about himself. So I said, "Whatever made you marry her?"

"Money," he said. But he said it too quickly. There was something in his tone which assured me that this disarming, frank admission was a lie. It was not that he seemed to expect me to doubt it, but that it seemed not to satisfy him entirely. His true reason must be something pretty shameful, I thought, if to claim this one was less painful to him. And then I knew what it was—to him far more shameful—he had married her because he loved her.

"She had a lot?" I asked.

"It seemed a lot to me at the time. It was during the crash, you see. I'd always made good money and when the crash came I laughed. We all did. Things would pick up in no time, so why worry. But things didn't and so—"

"So she came along with her gilt-edged securities and you saw your chance and took it."

"I married her," he said, and with those words the false tone was gone. "I think she had pretty well accustomed herself to the idea of staying single, being a career woman —or trying to become one. Only one man before me had ever had the nerve or the ignorance to buck her sister and propose to her. And you should have seen him. He was a florist. She showed me his picture once after we'd been married a while. In this picture he's on the boardwalk at Coney Island in an old-fashioned bathing suit down to his knees. He was about five feet tall and already bald all the way back to his ears. His name was Adelbert something. I think she meant to make me jealous by showing me his picture. Well, she didn't marry him because her sister objected, and she *did* marry me for the same reason. It was the first time in her life she ever crossed Victoria and for a while it made her feel she had done something heroic, defied everything for a great love."

He took a breath, then went on. "I spent the night before our wedding with this girl I was keeping. I guess you might say I'd decided to convince myself with one last fling that I had no regrets at leaving the single life behind. Anyhow, this girl had sort of dared me to do it and I did. Her name was Dolores. Dolores Davis. I still remember her quite well." (Evidently he thought this quite a feat of memory, considering, I supposed, how many had come since her.) "Alice believed I was out at a stag party too drunk to get to her place. To punish me she announced on our wedding night that she'd determined not to let me 'share her bed' for three months. She even marked down the exact date when I could begin to on a calendar—to torment me. That's the thing that's always got me. Alice never liked the business in bed, but she thought she ought to. It was the modern thing.

"In those days," he informed me in an aside, "people were beginning to talk about repression and all that sort of thing.

"I don't know how many women I've had since Dolores Davis. If you want to know," he said, "ask Alice. I'll bet she can tell you!"

. . . And so the spring wore on and the strange, perverse troubles of the Gavins wore on and I thought how many changes of the season had brought no change to them and I wondered why I thought it ever would.

One night Gavin took me to dinner to the house he kept in Webster's Bridge. There was something—something unpleasant, I grant—but at the same time something rather touchingly innocent in his way of reminding us every few minutes that we were all doing something we oughtn't to be. I felt embarrassed for Leila—not for the obvious reason, but because she seemed unaware how insignificant a place she, as a person in her own right, had in Gavin's heart, and I remember trying to help her out by arousing a spark of jealousy in him with questions about the husband she still had somewhere, though if he had been jealous of her he would have seen the eyes she was making at me.

VI

It must be hard, in keeping up an illusion, to be helped by the one person who has seen through it, no matter how sympathetic he may be. One morning, towards which I'd seen signs accumulating, Gavin allowed me to do all the talking, thereafter he responded but feebly to my reports of Alice's maneuvers, then I missed him for three days running and after that his participation in our game was no more than perfunctory and I began to miss him regularly every other day or so, both in the morning and in town at night, then for four or five days at a stretch, and at last for as long as two weeks together. I could imagine him picking up another newcomer, first accusing him of being a detective if not something more outlandish, and training him for my role.

Meanwhile Janice's father continued to ply me with gifts of fine cigars and rare books and old brandies, until she told him he would spoil my taste. He seemed to have had his answer in readiness. "No," he said, "I'll whet it." He must have. I got ambitious in the late spring and spent nights working overtime, and on one of those nights on the late train when I left my seat in the deserted coach and went out on the platform for a breath of air, I found Gavin. We must have stood for five minutes not three feet apart in the yellow light, he looking out one window at the night rushing past and I out the other, and then he recognized me first. Had he not I don't believe I would have known him at all. He was so changed that I know no way to express it but to say that now he looked his age. And though he was pleased to see me, his smile failed to enliven his face much, as it had done on a former occasion.

Our meetings had been ritualized before, and now I took his weariness and his pleasure at seeing me as a cue to begin again where we had left off. I said, "My, she must be really out to get you this time."

His reaction was slow. He thought for a moment with visible effort, apparently not knowing what I was talking about. Then he cried, "No!"

"No?" I echoed weakly.

And, seeing that I was not sure of it, that I had said it only to cheer him up, he laughed and said, "That old business is all over, Charley." There was a maturity in his tone which saddened me.

I remembered telling him once that like Dorian Gray he looked younger with each sin. Obsessed, desperate as his life had been, it was just what he had thrived on, it was what had kept him going. I felt guilty for having allowed him to tire of me. I said, "Hah! You're playing right into her hands. That's just what she intends—to lull you into complacency."

For a moment I thought I had reawakened him. For a moment the old fear came into his eyes. Then he said, "Nonsense. You're just trying to scare me."

We returned to the coach and when we were seated

he turned suddenly and caught me looking aggrievedly at the changes in his face and he said, "You're looking older, Charley."

It was not the irony of this which made me thoughtful. He had always been too self-absorbed to notice my looks or anything else about me. Our mutual interest had been him. Strange, to think that becoming less selfish could be a sign of a man's breaking up. He was all solicitude now and he presumed upon our friendship to hope earnestly that my marriage was working out well. And then he asked rather determinedly what I was doing out so late.

I said I had worked late.

Janice was a fine girl, he said.

I agreed.

He hoped I appreciated her, he said, with more than a shade of doubt in his look.

Now, just what had those few weeks since I'd seen him done? I asked after Alice, to which he replied in a tone from which I guessed that she was still alive, or that if she was dead that he hadn't heard about it, then I asked after Leila and he replied in the very same tone. I waited for an explanation.

"Oh, yes," he said. "You didn't know about that, did you? How long has it been since I saw you? Well, she and I broke up, oh, it must be, oh, five or six weeks ago." He was amazed, apparently, to realize that it was no longer ago. He wanted then to tell me something more, but something that he did not know how to lead up to, and finally he decided to dispense with any lead-up. "Well, about her," he said. "I've told Katherine about her, of course, but all the same—"

He paused and I nodded to show that I had explained Katherine to myself. But this did not altogether please

49

him. I had placed her, perhaps, a little too categorically.

"You get off with me at Webster's and come in for a while. Have dinner," he said.

It was no use my protesting the time. I had to see Katherine.

She was waiting for him, standing in the light of the doorway, waving. He stopped the car and she started out to meet him, but when she saw me get out of the car she stopped and, to my astonishment, grew quite flustered. Awkwardness was the last thing I expected—I can't tell you how long it was since I had seen a woman blush—and it was still less to be expected in a woman who looked like she did. For she was one of us, all right; such things as her relation with Gavin were not unheard-of to her; perhaps, indeed, she was what the women I knew only thought they were; there were depths of sophistication in her eyes and she carried herself in the approved way; she was knowing, chic—despite her innocent calico dress and her frilly little apron—but, as the evening taught me, there had remained an incorruptible simplicity in her and she filled her position with a refreshing un-ease.

No, she was not naturally the earnest, simple young matron sort, nor was their union, hers and Gavin's, the rocking-chair and reading-lamp and hassock-y kind which I saw through the open door. Things had changed here since Leila's time, and the thought of a life of sin in such ultra middle-class respectability had me ready to laugh aloud—until I caught Katherine's look as it came to me over Gavin's shoulder when he hugged her. That look told me what I should have known—that he, not she, was responsible for that room, that dress and that apron, and it warned me not to laugh.

50

She was that way, fiercely protective—even after he told her that I was his only friend—of his dream of domesticity, the sentimentality of which was simply incredible. He had to show me all of it, and it was like a trip through a Sears Roebuck catalogue: the kitchen, a vision of decalcomania and chintz, the silver service (Orange Blossom pattern), the newly redone knotty pine breakfast nook for two and the dining room for eight, the gadgets which were enough to make housekeeping a chore for Katherine—and throughout our tour I noticed her shy but determined affection for him and I approved her not letting my presence keep him from feeling it.

I was their first guest, so they treated me to all their accumulated hospitality. They treated me also to all the traditional foolery which newlyweds feel called upon to amuse older people with. There was a little skit in which he burlesqued his own easy householder air, one in which she demonstrated her wifely interest in his business day and her inability to understand the devious workings of the masculine world; then he tried to fix the iron which he must do if he were to have a clean shirt for tomorrow, and there was, of course, his disastrous attempt, in the costume of her apron, to mix the salad dressing.

While she prepared the dinner and he and I sat in the living room, he tried not to let me see how completely she absorbed him, tried to pay some attention to what I said, would engage me in earnest talk—only to break off and dash into the kitchen to get down from the shelf something for which she had only just begun to reach. And once he had to call me out there to show me that she had been about to put cinnamon on the asparagus, thinking it was pepper.

"She's nearsighted!" he said rapturously. He thought

this the most attractive, the most delightfully quaint, the most wondrously lovable quality any woman ever possessed —he had even made her feel it was something to be modest over—while she, it was apparent, thought herself inhumanly blessed to have got a man with twenty/twenty vision.

After dinner, over drinks, while they spared me only the minimum polite attention, I began to feel quite rosy. I was touched by the innocence and the sincerity of it, but more than that, by its being for Gavin so climacteric. I was beginning to feel quite paternal towards them, when suddenly . . .

"Mommy!"

It came from upstairs. It was all that was lacking. It was too much. I burst out laughing. Gavin looked at me reproachfully and he and Katherine exchanged stricken glances.

"I'll go," said Gavin.

It was the moving, Katherine explained. It still frightened Shirley to wake in a strange bedroom. "She's used to having me sleep with her," she said—then blushed violently.

Gavin, embarrassed at so much happiness, came down bearing a little girl who hugged him tightly and, ashamed of being seen in a crisis by a stranger, buried her face in his neck. When at last she was ready to be presented, Gavin introduced me as her Uncle Charley. Skeptical as she was of this sudden connection, even she, it seemed, had resolved to humor him.

He passed her to Katherine and sat looking at the picture they made and then suddenly his hospitality was at an end. "Your wife will be worried," he said in a tone which admitted no argument, and I supposed that in his

new state this was a thing he did not want to be responsible
for.

As he drove me home I watched his face in the glow of
the dashboard light. Perhaps it was only that I noticed it
for the first time then, but his face had undergone another
of those transformations of which it was so capable; it lost
years as the man in the ads loses his headache on taking
the pill. He was almost deliriously happy and he couldn't
get rid of me fast enough to carry out his determination.
And yet, he told me later, he had thought at one point
of taking me with him, to have someone to share his joy—
that was how little difficulty he foresaw and how little
need he felt for privacy when he asked Alice for a divorce.

He found a car in the drive, Victoria's car. This put
him out of his stride for just a moment, then he realized
that he could count upon her presence as a help. After
all, what had Victoria said for twenty years but that Alice
would do well to get rid of him? And if it occurred to him
to reckon the effect of Robert's presence, he dismissed it,
as anyone who knew Robert—or perhaps I should say, as
anyone who knew Victoria—was bound to do.

He was disappointed to find the fully lit drawing room
empty and it annoyed him to have to search for them. I
think he actually was impatient to share his enthusiasm
with them and when he burst into the studio where they
sat I believe he half-expected them to guess his state and
congratulate him.

He did not even pause over Alice's question, "Where
have you been?"

Then he began to notice with some surprise that the
looks on their faces were not friendly.

"Where have you been?" Alice repeated. "These ten
days."

He had actually forgotten how long it was since he had been home. In his late joy he had forgotten that he had another home in Cressett. Amazement over this was his first thought, then the full impact of Alice's question struck him. The irony of it was too much and he laughed. To gain a moment's time he strolled across the studio to the window, where, to look more at ease, he tapped out a rhythm on the drawing table. His fingers came back to him capped with dust. He looked at them slowly, then at the three faces. He saw Victoria smile faintly and he saw Alice flush. He knew then why Victoria was here and in Alice's face he saw what it had cost her to ask her sister to come.

Little was said by anyone. Their faces spoke for them. Gavin stood with his hopes still in his eyes and Victoria sat surveying him and Alice sat looking, as he told me later, very much as she had the first time he ever saw her. All Alice's professional dreams had at last deserted her and she had been brought sharply to face the fact of her age. She was bitter. All her resistances had been lowered and so when Gavin had not come home for ten days she had found herself vulnerable in some small but vital organ of female vanity that she never knew she had. She had become the helpless little spinster that he had married and she knew she had no one to fall back upon except Victoria. That was not going to be any soft cushion to fall back on, but something more like cold stone, and she was determined that if her rest henceforth was to be uneasy, Edward's would be, too. Victoria, she knew, had waited a long time for this; one whipping post, Robert, had never given her the workout she needed daily, and Alice was determined that for every lash she felt she would make Edward feel

54

two. He had something now that he really wanted, something through which she could hurt him.

She did not want him back. Marrying him in the first place had meant for her that she no longer needed a husband. He had never suited her anyhow. She would have liked a husband like Robert, one who allowed himself to be made over into a kind of decorative, thoroughbred-looking hearth dog.

It was Robert's face which said the most to Gavin. For Robert had always hated him and Gavin knew it and knew why and now he saw that he would have to pay for his difference, those twenty years of independence, for Robert meant not to leave him a shirt to his back.

VII

I see Gavin now and again on the train and sometimes we ride together, but I can't be much company to him now, he doesn't need anybody to stimulate any mock fears in him any more, and he feels bad that he is no more company to me. He is aging badly and the strain of trying to lead a double life—that is, to include his legal one—is beginning to tell. He never tried to make his excuses convincing before, so now when he does steal a night away for himself, for Katherine, he has trouble thinking up what to tell Alice. He has softened a great deal towards Alice. No doubt this is partly tactical but mostly it is genuine. He knows now how much she missed in life and he is tender with her. But no matter what he does it's wrong; when he comes home nights she is more suspicious than when he stays away, his excuses confirm her suspicions and his kindness leaves her no doubt at all.

I tell him every time I see him to get out of that house

in Webster's Bridge and he agrees vacantly but does nothing about it. Lately I've even seen him get off the train there again and just last night I was sure I saw Robert Hines follow him off there. He likes the place. It is the scene of all his happiness. He likes to recall what it was to him before Katherine and to contrast that with his present love. Perhaps he still tries to convince himself that they won't think to look so near home. But at bottom it is hopelessness that keeps him there. What he had found at last seemed to him from the start too good to last and he is convinced that to move would merely postpone the inevitable end of a happiness which is more than he deserves.

The Shell

~~~~~~

T his would be the season, the year, when he
would have the reach of arm to snap the big
gun easily to his shoulder. This fall his shoulder would not
be bruised black from the recoil. The hunting coat would
fit him this season. This would be *the* season—the season
when he would have to shoot the shell.

It was a twelve-gauge shotgun shell. The brass was green
with verdigris, the cardboard, once red, was faded to a pale
and mottled brown, the color of old dried blood. He knew
it intimately. On top, the firing cap was circled by the
loop of a letter *P*. Around the rim, circling the *P*, were the
two words of the trade name, *Peters Victor*; the gauge
number, 12; and the words, *Made in USA*. The wad inside the crimp of the firing end read, *Smokeless*; $3\frac{1}{4}$;
$1\frac{1}{8}$-8. This meant $3\frac{1}{4}$ drams of smokeless powder, $1\frac{1}{8}$
ounces of number 8 shot—birdshot, the size for quail. It
was the one shell he had found afterwards that had belonged to his father, one that his father had not lived to
shoot. So he had thought at first to keep the shell unfired.
But he knew his father would have said that a shotgun
shell was meant to be fired, and he, Joe, had added that
any shotgun shell which had belonged to him was meant

57

to hit what it was fired at. For four years now it had been out of Joe's pocket, and out of his hand fingering it inside his pocket, only to stand upon the table by his bed at night. For four years now he had been going to shoot it when he was good enough, but the better he became the further away that seemed to get, because good enough meant, though he did not dare put it to himself in quite that way, as good as his father had been.

He had been in no great rush about it during those first two seasons afterwards, then there had been time—though now it seemed that even then there had been less time than he admitted. But on opening day of the third, last year's season, he had suddenly found himself sixteen years old—for though his birthday came in May, it was in November, on opening day of quail season, that he really began another year—time was suddenly short, and then overnight gone completely, after that day when he returned with the best bag he had ever taken and, in his cockiness, had told his mother about the shell, what he had saved it for and what he meant to do with it.

He had not allowed himself to forget that at that moment he could hear his father saying, "Do it and then talk about it." He had argued weakly in reply that he was telling only his mother, and then it was not his father but the voice of his own conscience which had cried, "Only!" Because whom alone did he want to tell, to boast to, and because already he knew that that was not what his father would have said, but rather, "Do it and don't talk about it afterwards either."

She had seemed hardly surprised to learn about the shell. She seemed almost to have known about it, expected it. But she handled it reverently because she could see that he did.

"Aren't you good enough now?" she said.

"Hah!" he said.

She was turning the shell in her fingers. "I always knew nothing would ever happen to him while hunting," she said. "I never worried when he was out with a gun . . . Well," she brought herself up, "but I worry about you. Oh, I know you're good with a gun. I'm not afraid you'll hurt yourself."

"Not with the training I've had," he said.

"No," she said. "What I worry about is the amount of time and thought you give it. Are you keeping up in school? The way you go at it, Joe! It hardly even seems to be a pleasure to you."

Pleasure? No, it was not a pleasure, he thought. That was the name he had always given it, but he was older now and no longer had to give the name pleasure to it. Sometimes—often times when he enjoyed it most—it was the opposite of pleasure. What was the proper name for it? He did not know. It was just what he did, the thing he would have been unable to stop doing if he had wanted to; it was what he was.

"I see other boys and girls your age going out to picnics and parties, Joe. I'm sure it's not that you're never invited."

"You know that kind of thing don't interest me," he said impatiently.

She was serious for a moment and said, "You're so old for your age, Joe. Losing your father so young." Then she altered, forced her tone. "Well, of course, you probably know exactly what you're up to," she said. "It's the hunters the girls really go for, isn't it? Us girls—us Southern girls—like a hunting man! I did. I'll bet all the little girls just—"

He hated it when she talked like that. She knew that

59

girls meant nothing to him. He liked it when she let him know that she was glad they didn't. He liked to think that when she teased him this way it was to get him to re-affirm how little he cared for girls; and yet she should know that his feeling for her was, like the feeling he had for hunting, too deep a thing for him to be teased into declaring.

He took the shell away from her.

"You're good enough now," she said.

"No," he said sullenly. "I'm not."

"He would think so."

"I don't think so. I don't think he would."

"I think so. You're good enough for me," she said.

"No. No, I'm not. Don't say that," he said.

He was in the field at daybreak on opening day with Mac, the speckled setter, the only one of his father's dogs left now, the one who in the three seasons he had hunted him had grown to be his father's favorite, whom he had broken that season that he had trained, broken, him, Joe, too, so that between him and the dog, since, a bond had existed less like that of master to beast, more like that of brother to brother, and consequently, he knew, he had never had the dog's final respect and did not have it now, though the coat did fit now.

He had not unleashed the dog yet, but stood with him among the bare alders at the edge of the broom grass meadow that had the blackened pile of sawdust in the middle—the color of fresh cornmeal the first time he ever saw it—to which he, and the big covey of quail, went first each season, the covey which he had certainly not depleted much but which instead had grown since his father's death.

The coat fit now, all right, but he wore it still without

presumption, if anything with greater dread and with even less sense of possession than when it came halfway down to his knees and the sleeves hung down to the midjoints of his fingers and the armpits looped nearly to his waist and made it absolutely impossible to get the gun stock to his shoulder, even if he could have lifted the big gun there in that split second when the feathered balls exploded at his feet and streaked into the air. He had not worn the coat then because he believed he was ready to wear it nor hunted with the big gun because he believed he was the man to. He had not been ready for a lot of things, had had to learn to drive, and drive those first two years seated on a cushion to see over the hood; he had not been ready to sit at the head of the table, to carve the meat, to be the comforter and protector, the man of the house. He had had to wear the coat and shoot the gun and rock on his heels and just grit his teeth at the kick, the recoil.

Maybe there had been moments later—the day he threw away the car cushion was one—when he was pleased to think that he was growing into the coat, but now, as he stood with Mac, hunching and dropping his shoulders and expanding his chest inside it, it seemed to have come to fit him before he was at all prepared for it to. He heard the loose shells rattle in the shell pockets and he smelled the smell of his father, which now, four years later, still clung to it, or else what he smelled was the never-fading, peppery smell of game blood and the clinging smell of gunpowder, the smell of gun oil and the smell of the dog, all mixed on the base of damp, heavy, chill November air, the air of a quail-shooting day, the smells which had gone to make up the smell his father had had for him. Reaching his hand into the shell pocket he felt something clinging in the seam. It was a faded, tangled and blood-stiffened pinfeather of a quail. It was from a bird his father had shot. He himself had never killed so many that the game pockets would not hold them all and he had had to put them in the shell pockets.

He took from among the bright other ones *the* shell and slipped it into the magazine and pumped it into the breech. He would have to make good his boast to his mother, though he knew now that it was a boast made no more out of cockiness than cowardice and the determination born of that cowardice to fix something he could not go back on. He would have to fire the shell today. He had known so all the days as opening day approached. He had known it at breakfast in the lighted kitchen with his mother, remembering the times when she and himself had sat in the lighted kitchen over breakfast on opening day with his father, both in the years when he himself had stayed behind and watched his father drive away into the just-breaking dawn, not even daring yet to yearn for his own time to come, and later when he began to be taken; he had seen it in the dog, Mac's eyes as he put him into the cage, the dog cage his father had had built into the car trunk though it was the family car, the only one they had to go visiting in as well, that he would have to fire the shell today, and he had known it most as he backed out of the drive and waved good-by to his mother, remembering the times when his father had been in the driver's seat and she had stood waving to the two of them.

Now he felt the leash strain against his belt loop and heard the dog whimpering, and out in the field, rising liquid and clear into the liquid air, he heard the first bob-white and immediately heard a second call in answer from across the field and the first answer back, and then, as though they had tuned up to each other, the two of them fell into a beat, set up a round-song of alternate call and response: bob bob white white, bob bob white white, and then others tuned in until there were five, eight separate and distinctly timed voices, and Joe shivered, not ashamed of his emotion and not trying to tell himself it was the cold, but owning that it was the thrill which nothing else, not even other kinds of hunting, could ever give him and which not even his dread that it was the day when he would have to shoot the shell could take away from him, and knowing for just that one moment that this was the real, the right feeling to have, that it was the coming and trying that mattered, the beginning, not the end of the day, the empty, not the full game pockets, feeling for just that moment in deep accord with his father's spirit, feeling him there with him, beside him, listening, loading up, unleashing the dog.

As soon as the dog was unleashed his whimpering ceased. Joe filled the magazine of the gun with the two ordinary shells and stood rubbing the breech of the gun, watching the dog enter the field. He veered instantly and began systematically quartering the field, his nose high and loose, on no fresh scent yet, but quickening, ranging faster already. They claimed—and of most dogs it was true —that setters forgot their training between seasons, but not Mac, not the dog his father had trained, not even after three seasons, even with no better master than him to keep him in training. He watched him now in the field lower his muzzle slightly as the scent freshened and marveled at the style the dog had, yet remembered paradoxically that first day, his and Mac's, when each of them, the raw, noisy, unpromising-looking pup and the raw, unpromising-looking but anything but noisy boy, had flushed birds, the pup a single but he a whole covey—two of which his father had bagged nonetheless—for which the pup had received a beating and he only a look, not even a scolding look, but a disappointed look worse than any beating he had ever had.

The dog set: broke stride, lowered his muzzle, then planted all four feet as though on the last half-inch of a sudden and unexpected cliff-edge, raised his muzzle and leaned forward into the scent streaming hot and fresh into his nostrils, leaned his whole body so far forward that the raised, rigid, feathered tail seemed necessary as a ballast to keep him from falling on his face. You could tell from his manner that it was the whole big covey.

He called as he set out down the field. "Steady, boy. Toho," he called, and on the dead misty air his voice did not seem his voice at all but his father's voice, calling as he had heard him call, and he was struck afresh and more powerfully than ever before with the sense of his own unworthiness, his unpreparedness, which seemed now all the more glaringly shown forth by the very nearness he had attained to being prepared; he felt himself a pretender, a callow and clownish usurper.

Now the birds were moving, running in the cover, still banded together, and Mac moved up his stand, so cautiously that he seemed jointless with rigidity. Stock-still, trembling with controlled excitement, his eyes glazed and the hair along his spine bristling, you could have fired an artillery piece an inch above his head and still he would have stood unflinching for an hour, until told to break his stand, and so Joe let him stand, to enjoy the sight, as well as to give his pounding heart a moment's calm, before going in to kick them up. He held the gun half-raised, and the shell in the barrel seemed to have increased its weight tenfold. Alongside the dog he said again, "Steady, boy," knowing that this time he spoke not to the dog but to himself.

It was as if he had kicked the detonator of a land mine. There was a roaring whir as the birds, twenty of them at least, burst from the grass at his feet like hurtling fragments of shell and gouts of exploding earth, flung up and out and rapidly diminishing in a flat trajectory, sailing earthward almost instantly, as if, though small, deceptively heavy and traveling with incredible velocity.

The gun went automatically to his shoulder, snapped up there more quickly and gracefully than ever before. He had a bird in his eye down the barrel and knew that he had got it there quickly enough to get a second shot easily. But his breath left him as though knocked out by the burst and pounding rush of wings. Fear that he might miss, miss with *the* shell, paralyzed him. He lowered the gun unfired. Turning to the still-rigid dog, he saw—as one in such case is always liable to see on the face of a good bird dog—his look of bewildered disappointment. In that instant it seemed to Joe that the fear of finding just that look was what had unnerved him, and though he was ashamed of the impulse, all his own disappointment and self-contempt centered in hatred for the dog.

As soon as he was given leave, Mac went after the singles. He set on one instantly.

Joe kicked up this single and again the anxiety that he might miss, such that sweat filled his armpits and he felt his mouth go dry, overcame him, and with trembling hands he had to lower the hammer and lower the gun unfired, and was unable to face the dog.

He tried on three more singles. It got worse. He knew then without looking at him that Mac had given him up and would refuse to hunt any more today. He did not even have to put him on the leash. The dog led the way out of the field. Joe found him lying at the rear of the car, and he did not need even to be told, much less dragged, as usual with him on any shooting day but especially on opening day, to get into the cage to go home.

The lemon pie was in the refrigerator, the marshmallow-topped whipped yams in the oven and the biscuits cut and in the pan and on the cabinet waiting to go into the oven the moment the birds were plucked—all as it always was when his father returned in the evening of a quail-shooting day, and as it was later when he and his father, and still later when he came home alone and laid the dead birds in her lap, as he had laid the first dollar he ever earned.

She said, cheerfully, that it was a lucky thing she happened to have some chops in the house. She added that she had learned that long ago. A woman learned, she said, never to trust to a hunter's luck—not even the best hunter. He was both grateful and resentful of those words. He knew she had never bought meat against his father's coming home from a hunt empty-handed.

He rested a day, went to school a week, and practiced, shooting turnips tossed into the air and hitting five out of seven, then he went back. The quail were there, you could hear them, but when he looked at Mac as he was about to loose him and felt himself quaking already, he snapped the leash on again and went back to the car and home.

And so what it turned into, this season for which he finally had the reach and the size, the endurance, in a word the manliness, was the one in which he fired no shell at all.

The Thanksgiving holidays came and he spent every day in the field with the shell in the barrel of the gun—a few bright brass nicks in the dull green now where the ejector had gripped pumping it in and out of the breech—and the magazine full behind it of his own waiting shells and with Mac. He hardly spoke to the dog now, gave him no commands and no encouragements, nor did the dog give tongue or whimper or even frisk, a kind of wordless and even gestureless rapport between them, the two of them hunting now in a grim, cold fury of impotence.

The dog had gone past disappointment, past disgust, past even bewilderment, and seemed now to have divined the reason or else the irresistible lack of all reason behind the coveys kicked up, the boy—almost the man now—raising and cocking his gun, but shaking his head even as he raised it, holding it erect and steady on his mark, then lowering it slowly and soundlessly and releasing him from stand and hunting on. His mother gave up trying to keep him at home, and seemed to have sensed the desperate urgency in him.

And now as the days passed and closing day of the season neared he could feel the whole town watching him, awaiting the climax of his single-minded pursuit, their curiosity first aroused by what they would have been most certain to observe: the lack of interest which they would think he should have begun to show in girls. The boys had noticed, had taken to gathering in a body on his shift at the Greek's confectionery at night, ordering him to make sodas for them and their dates, and ribbing him.

"Haven't seen much of you lately, Joe. Where you been?"

"Around."

"Yeah, but around who?"

Guffaws.

"I've been busy."

"I'll bet you have, old Joe."

Titters.

"Busy. Yeah."

Then he would blush. "I've been hunting," he said.

"I'll bet you have!"

He blushed again and said—he could never learn to avoid that kind of double meaning—"Quail."

They roared. "Getting many?" they said, and "Aren't we all?" and "Watch out for those San Quentin quail," they said.

Everybody knew everybody else's business in town anyhow, and moreover he was a kind of public figure in his way—they could not have helped but watch the coming-of-age of the son of the greatest wing shot the town ever had —so that he felt now that the ear of the whole town was cupped to hear the report of the shell, a sound which to him it had come to seem would have no resemblance whatever to the noise of any other shotgun shot ever heard.

At nights he studied the shell, trying to discover the source of its charm. He had come to fear it, almost to hate it, certainly to live by and for it.

How can you, he asked himself—no, he could make the question general, for he asked it not self-ironically but just incredulously—how can a boy want to be better than his father? Not better. It was not that. Not even as good as. That was not what he wanted at all. What was it? It was that you wanted to *be* your father, wasn't it? Yes, that was it. That was more what it was. And you weren't.

But wasn't there just a little bit of wanting to be better than, mixed in with it? Wasn't there, in fact, just a little bit of thinking you *were* better than, mixed in with it? All right, yes. Yes, there was. Why? It was because you believed that being half him you had all he was, and being half your mother you had that much again that he wasn't, that he did not have. And you knew that he would have agreed with this, which did not make you believe it entirely, or stop believing it.

Then it was closing day. The big covey was long gone from the broom grass meadow now, ranging from the swamps and brier patches to the uplands and the loblolly pines at the thicket edges. You had to work to find them now and any shot you got was likely to be a snap shot, through branches or brush. But this was how he wanted it. Let it get hard enough and it would be *the* shot and he would take it.

There were no waiting shells in the magazine of the gun today. He wanted no second shot, at least not on the same flush.

It was about eight in the morning when Mac got a warm scent. Did he know it was closing day? You would think so from the way he had suddenly taken cheer—or hysteria —determination, certainly. His spirits were not dampened even by the lowering of the unfired gun at the first single he found. He seemed in agreement that this one had been too easy.

They were hunting in uplands, in blackened stover bent to the ground and frozen, so that it snapped against Joe's boots. Then Mac headed down out of the cornfield, crossed a fencerow and was in a swamp, in sedge, tall and dead and bent. Joe could follow Mac, as 'way ahead of him the tall stiffened grass parted and closed heavily behind the dog's passage. Then he could not follow him any more and he whistled, and when he got no answer he knew that the dog had set and could not give tongue.

He began to rush, though he knew that Mac would

hold or follow the birds. Feeding time for the birds was almost over. They would be drifting toward the thickets now and in another hour would go deep into the pines and then the dog could not hunt them, no dog. Then the hunting would not be good again until nightfall and that was the very last chance. It had better be now.

The bog continued for as far as he could see in the milky mist and he stood for a moment wishing the dog would give tongue just once, knowing that he was too well trained, and then he decided to go left, south. The land soon began to rise and the sedge got shorter and soon he could see where the swamp gave out at a fencerow and beyond that he soon could see a clearing rising out of the fog and rising up into pine woods. He could see no sign of the dog, but that was where he was sure to be.

He climbed over the barbwire, still looking ahead up into the clearing, and bent to get through the briers and came out with his head still raised looking up and almost stepped on the rigid, unbreathing dog, his nose in the wind, pointed as stiff as a weathervane.

He cocked the gun and stepped into the brush and kicked. They roared out toward the pines. He swung on his heel, holding the gun half-raised, picking his bird. He swiveled a half-circle, twisted at the waist, and saw the big cock, big as a barnyard rooster, streaking for the pines. He shot. The sound seemed to go beyond sound, one of those the hearer does not hear because the percussion has instantly deafened him, and he felt himself stagger from the recoil. But down the barrel of the gun he saw the bird, pitching for the ground at the thicket edge, winging along untouched, without a feather ruffled, and he knew that he had missed. From old habit he was already pumping the gun, and it was when he saw the big shell flick out and spin heavily into the brush that he realized he had heard no sound but a light dry click. The shell had not gone off. The shell was a dud. He had kept it too long; it had gone dead.

He said it aloud. "I have kept it too long. It's a dud."

Then he felt himself soaring as though in a burst of wings like the cock bird, as though he had been shot at himself and gone unscatched, free.

He dropped the shell into his pocket. It would rest permanently on his bureau now, he had time to tell himself. Then he was fumbling for fresh shells, his own shells, and dropping them all over the ground at his feet and getting one into the chamber backwards and saying to Mac in a voice he could just recognize as his own, "All right, don't stand there! Go get 'em! Go get 'em, boy! Go get 'em!" And he could tell that Mac knew it was his master's voice speaking now, a hunter's voice.

In Sickness and Health

~~~~~~

Mr. Grogan's bald head broke through the covers. He experimented with his nose; it rattled like steampipes warming up. He was so stiff he felt that all the veins in his body must have froze and busted. He opened his eyes and wriggled painfully upwards, feeling, after only one day in bed, stiff and strange as an old snake crawling out of hibernation. Now, if only he had stayed on his feet, as he had insisted, he would have been feeling hearty again this morning.

He could hear his wife down below walloping up his breakfast, doubtless assuring herself that he was so near dead he would never hear her, murmuring soft little Viennese curses whenever her big hulk smacked into the cabinet corner. Mr. Grogan licked a fingertip and scrubbed the corners of his eyes. When she came up he would look long awake, though he had not been able to get up.

Mr. Grogan was an early riser. You couldn't tell her otherwise, and his wife had the notion he did it to make her look lazy. He just wanted to get out of a morning without the sight of her. Maybe she was brighter than he took her for, and just as spiteful as he knew she was, and wanted to rob him of that pleasure. One reason or another, she was to be heard scrambling and puffing in the mornings, trying to get down before he did, and now he could just imagine how pleased with herself she was today.

He knew just how her mind was working. Had she stopped to consider that he just might be better this morning? Not for an instant. She was too cheerful down there now for such a shadow to have passed even momentarily across her mind. An hour at least she must have lolled abed this morning, thinking to herself how, even after time for the alarm, she might go right on lying there as long as she pleased, and still be the first down in the kitchen. No racing down this morning, no colliding in the hall, no frowzy hair nor unlaced shoes, all to see which one—and he it was just about always—could be sitting there already polishing off his coffee with a distant, foregone glance for the stay-a-bed. Yes, she had that kind of a nasty mind.

The breakfast she came up with would have winded a slender woman.

"Ah, *liebchen*, no better, hah?" she grinned, and when he opened his mouth to remonstrate, she drew a concealed thermometer and poked it in him.

Mr. Grogan lay there with it poked out defiantly at her, making it seem there was so much of her that he had to look first around one side of it, then around the other, to take her all in. She stood over him regally; she did every chance she got. Mrs. Grogan carried her head with great pride of ownership, as though she had shot it in Ceylon and had it mounted on a plaque.

She must have thought that the longer she left the thermometer in, the higher it would go. He started to take it out, but she beat him to it.

"Ah!" she sighed, regarding it with deep satisfaction. "Ah-hah!"

Nothing could have made Mr. Grogan ask her what it said. Not even if he had believed she knew how to read the thing.

"That's what you need," she said. "Plenty sleep and decent food," and the way she said it you would think she had found him in a doorway in the Bowery and given him the only home he had ever known.

"Well, you don't," he replied, but she was gone. Amazing, truly, how fast she could move that great body of hers when it meant getting out in time to have the last word herself.

He could hear her vast sigh as she stood at the head of the basement steps. He could hear her settle slowly down the steps, then scrape her way over to the coalbin. There was no subtlety in her, and that was what he resented most. There she went now, rattling the furnace. She might be Mrs. Beelzebub opening shop. Soon she would come up to demonstrate her pains, complaining of the heat, the dirt, the waste of coal. Were he to dare remind her that *he*, certainly, required no fire, why, she would burst. What would she have done for heat if he hadn't come down like this? Last winter she had practically turned blue before she would ask him to build a fire. But that had not taught her, and this time she would have moved out sooner than admit she was cold—though how she could get cold through all her insulation was more than he could guess. But cold she was, stiff as untried lard, while here was himself with his hundred and twenty pounds, and that old and ailing, and all along he might have been a teapot in a cozy, he told himself—while the yellowed old teeth danced in his mouth like popcorn in a pan.

75

She stood at the door, grateful for having made the stairs once again. She had been sure to get good and smeared with soot and coal dust, and not stop to wash any of it. Mr. Grogan had thrown back two of his blankets and was smoking the pipe she had forbidden him, though he did not dare inhale for fear of a coughing spell. So smug she looked, turning up his radiator, her sleeves rolled back, just stifling for the sake of his health. He could not resist asking, "Would you mind just raising up that window there while you're close by?" She turned on him such a smile as she might have given a child she was holding for ransom.

After that she left him alone. Maybe she was thinking that alone he would come to enjoy a nice warm room, a day in bed with meals brought up, realize how much he did owe her to be sure. But even if it were pleasant would she let a man enjoy it? And on that sour thought his pipe drained in his mouth and started a coughing fit that very nearly choked him in trying to keep her from hearing. Ah, Grogan, he chided himself, wouldn't it have been better now to have built a fire back in November and worn the muffler like she said? A stubborn, wheezing "no!" shot through him. But wouldn't it now? Didn't he regret the false front of good health and didn't he wish he had confessed to sniffles three days ago and staved off what was sure to develop into pneumonia?

Come now. Were things that black, truly? Well, he was not exactly what you would call hale, but nobody but himself would ever know it, and better by far than she gave him the credit for. He still cut a pretty sturdy figure and nobody ever heard him complain. In fact, he had been maybe a little too uncomplaining. Well, if so he could point out where to lay the blame. What else could a man do only swallow down his aches and pains, never mention them nor so much as let them be guessed, when he knew that if they were her face would light up at every hole like a new candle had been put in it. Many the time he had felt so bad that younger men than he by years would have spent the week in bed and he had got right up—first, too, more like than not—made his own breakfast, it went without saying, and gone to work with a smile and a tipped hat for everybody on the street.

Meanwhile she had been giving him a standing with the neighbors that she never dreamed was noble. "Oh, I'm very well, Mrs. Harriman, very well indeed. It's Mr. Grogan, you know." This she would sadly volunteer over the back fence. She had to volunteer it, for no one ever thought to *ask* after such a chipper man. In those days Mr. Grogan got no end of delight in knowing that to Mrs. Harriman and to the rest of the neighbors, his wife was making of herself either a liar or a lunatic. For whenever he caught sight of her on the back fence speaking with Mrs. Harriman and looking sadly up at his window, then he would rush out and start weeding his garden in a flaming fury. Or he would trot down the street and catch flies as the kids played baseball, wind up and burn the ball home. He just wished she could have seen the neighbors' faces then!

But people are always anxious to believe the worst about someone else's health. The neighbors then respected him, stood aside on the walks, offered little services and some of them went so far as to consult him about their own illnesses, he being such a fine example of how to bear so many. Then he may have peacocked it a bit; he supposed he did. Not that he wanted their attention. If he played up to all this ever so little it was because it was pleasant to see her program turning out so different from the way she had planned it.

Soon, though, it got to looking like they were saying among themselves, "Well, here comes that poor half-dead fool Grogan, with no idea of all that's going on inside hisself." There did seem to be such a conspiracy against him, he had thought more than once of taking a loss on his equity in the house and finding a new neighborhood. Hereabouts just to walk down the block of an afternoon made him feel the morgue had given him a day off his slab.

Now another situation held among Mr. Grogan's friends and it was only this that kept him going. Mr. Grogan was a great one for broadening himself with new friends and he was attracted naturally and by principle to young men. The few friends his wife had managed to keep were as old and mostly older than herself. Her claim was that he palled around with his young friends in a vain and unbecoming attempt to imagine himself their age again. But this, he knew, was to cover her own guilt for avoiding all younger women that she might not appear any older by contrast, and comparing her own fine fat state daily to the failing energies of her old crones.

Mr. Grogan prided himself on the job he had done of keeping his friends away from his wife. They, then, had no reason for not taking his word that he enjoyed excellent health. Not one of them but would have had trouble believing otherwise of anybody, and when he was with them Mr. Grogan never felt an ache or a pain. So, it was shocking to slip like a ghost down the three blocks nearest his house, turn the corner and enter McLeary's tavern like the playboy of Western Long Island.

Just the kind of a shock Mr. Grogan would have welcomed when toward eleven o'clock there came up to him the sound of substantial steps on the back stoop and he heard his wife greet her friend Mr. Rauschning, the baker. Into the kitchen they would go, where she would stuff him with the marzipan she bought from him at cutthroat prices, so Mr. Grogan expected, but instead he heard them on the steps up to his room and the two of them rumbled in like a Panzer division.

Mr. Rauschning took one look at him. Then he removed the cigar from his mouth and turned it over and over, squinting at it as though he could read his temperature on it and was satisfied that it could never be as alarming as Grogan's. "*Ja*," he said, and to this Mrs. Grogan nodded gravely.

Neighborhood kids said that Rauschning soured his dough by scowling at it. But to Mr. Grogan he was no surlier than the rest of his compatriots. To Mr. Grogan it seemed his wife's friends wore a look of petty insolence, to which he contrasted the noble defiance of generations of Irishmen oppressed by the same grievance.

"Since yesterday morning," his wife commented on his condition, and Rauschning nodded; he could have predicted it to the hour.

"And the *Herr Doktor*, what does he say?"

"Hah! What doctor?"

Mr. Rauschning said ah-hah. Between them his fate was sealed.

"Well, how's the bakery business?" Mr. Grogan inquired amiably, and wished he hadn't as Rauschning nodded faintly to a man who would soon have little concern over the staff of life.

"Well, Grogan, I hope you get better," he said, and turned back at the door to add, "soon." He turned then to Mrs. Grogan to indicate that his anxiety was for her, as well as his condolences—for hopes, before such evidence, were vain, ending with a smile of agreement that she would be better off afterwards, of course, for a good strong German woman would always get by.

Now they were gone and Mr. Grogan thought he would just forget they were ever there, doze off wishing the two of them off on one another. But that would suit her too well. Ah, how often had she wished aloud for the likes of him herself, him or her first husband back again, whose speckled portrait sat on her bureau fading a little more each year as though still fleeing the vigor of her tongue.

The two dearest friends Mrs. Grogan owned came around noon to have the invalid exhibited to them. His wife must have phoned everybody she knew the night before when she had him drugged asleep, urged them all over for a laugh. But there stirred in him suddenly a fear that something unmistakably desperate in his appearance that was plain to all but him, something that they figured would this morning come to an inevitable crisis, something that had escaped him while draining away his very life, something horrible had summoned them all this morning with no help from her necessary. Was it possible? Had she been right all along, sincere, and the neighbors, had they honestly seen it coming?

They came up while he was feeling himself frantically for ailments he might have overlooked. They were Miss Hinkle and Mrs. Schlegelin and it was easy to see how even Mrs. Grogan could feel secure in their company. Miss Hinkle came in with a twitter at being in a man's bedroom and Mrs. Grogan was astonished that she could feel that way in the bedroom of a man with so little of his manhood left him. The sight of Mrs. Schlegelin could make

Mr. Grogan feel there was hope for even him, for who ever saw such a thing so skinny from head to toe?

"Like the flu looks maybe," she diagnosed. "Just like *mein* Helmut exactly when he came down mit flu."

Mr. Grogan snorted, thinking how much more than flu he would have to have to look at all like her Helmut.

Miss Hinkle, terrified that she might catch sight of a bedpan, squealed, "Elsa, smells here like in Germany in the epidemic, ain't it?"

"Hush, Hedvig, no," shooshed Mrs. Schlegelin, her nose climbing up her face, and Miss Hinkle sniggered.

And they said other things, even after Mr. Grogan slowly flourished from the drawer of his nightstand two abandoned wads of chewing gum—really two waxen cotton plugs—and screwed them into his ears.

A tactic he had developed some time back. Mr. Grogan disliked using it, it made for all sorts of trouble, but was surely called for now. Wax-treated cotton they were, soft, easily got in, and they set like cement. Twenty-five cents a month bought a private little world all his own. Herself resented the price. With a display of thrift and resourcefulness, she bought a roll of cotton big enough for quilting, a tin of tallow, and made her own. She looked to be troubled with his voice for even longer than he ever hoped. For a while it piqued him. Now he simply had to laugh. One of many examples it became of her racial penny-wiseness—because he could make himself heard to her with but the tiniest elevation of his ordinary tone, while she had to shout herself hoarse.

You could not insult them. They left, but not before they were ready. But they might have spent the night for all of Emmett Grogan. He was sealed in, with smiles rising up like bubbles in new wine. But try as he might there was no convincing himself that this solitude was at all what he wanted. He was lonely in there. And he feared that these last two were not the last by any means. A long list of Mrs. Grogan's acquaintances rolled across his mind, the two down in the kitchen being welcome compared to some. He uncorked one ear and a dull whistle of Platt-deutsch rushed in.

Mr. Grogan gave himself a shake to unstick a joint or two, threw the covers back and carefully watched himself get up, afraid of leaving something behind. Sadly he wrenched himself out of his nightgown. Once in his pants he knew how much he had shrunk. Breaking up, he could see it in the mirror. But it was never a clear glass, and the light poorly, and moreover it was a man had spent a day in bed. Lying there that way the flesh slid of its own weight off the bones in front and would take time to get properly rearranged. He would know in McLeary's tavern. Someone would be sure to remark, "Grogan, you're not looking your-self"—which he was bound to admit, that is, not looking *himself*, meaning that a slight change in a ruddy face was enough for decent well-meant concern that never for a minute overstated the case.

Down the steps stealthily went Mr. Grogan that his wife would not hear the labor it cost him, his eyes steady on the landing where he planned a rest, but as he reached it his wife brought her guests from the kitchen to see them out the front door. From somewhere he dug up the energy to trot briskly by.

"Don't wait supper on me," he flung at her without so much as a glance over his shoulder. And his little spurt of exertion turned out to be the very thing he had been needing. He knew all along it was.

Housewives were indoors, children in school, dogs in

kennels, Ireland still in the Atlantic and Germany in ruins and Emmett Grogan was in the street. Natural phenomena all. There was a list to his step that passed for a swagger as he crashed the door at McLeary's. The place was deserted. McLeary hung over a scratch sheet at the far end of the bar and he tucked it grudgingly away while Mr. Grogan ascended a stool. Somebody had surely pickled McLeary as a foetus, but he had kept growing, had been lately discovered, spilled out and set going. Little half-opened eyes were getting a start in his squashed face, he was adenoidal, potbellied, but to Mr. Grogan he looked good.

"Leave the bottle?" he asked after pouring a shot, to which Mr. Grogan nodded carelessly. McLeary went back immediately to his scratch sheet. Mr. Grogan tamped another down, and felt his insides warm and expand. He got down from his stool, looked annoyed with the sunlight at his end of the counter, and moved with his bottle down nearer McLeary.

"Something else, Mr. Grogan?"

"No. No, nothing further, thank you, McLeary. This will do it if anything will, I suppose."

"Something amiss, Mr. Grogan?"

"Ah, nothing serious, you understand. Nasty little bit of a cold."

"Ah, yes. Too bad. There's an epidemic, so I understand."

That was conserving your sympathy, spreading it pretty thin. Starting on another tack, he asked, "Where could everybody be this fine day?"

"Not here," McLeary observed sourly.

"What can it be, do you suppose?"

McLeary shrugged; he was unable to imagine a counter-attraction so strong.

Grogan pushed away his bottle. "And I'll be having a beer to help that on its way, if you please, McLeary." He was determined to stick it out until some friend came in. But he had had whisky enough and more, and he always did get a guilty feeling sitting empty-handed in a bar.

To go home again would have robbed the venture of all its worth. But he did not like to think of it as a venture. He would like to feel he could go home when he pleased, for after all he had done nothing unusual—got well, got up. No point to be proved to anybody. All too subtle for her, however. She would get the idea he hadn't been able to stand on his feet any longer. She would have something there, too, but his unsteadiness came from good healthy rye whisky.

Grogan, a voice pulled him down by the ear, you're not feeling well and you know it. Naturally, he replied, I've been sick, what do you expect. You're sick and getting sicker. No, drunk and getting drunker. Mr. Grogan decided to take his stomach out for an airing. Would drop in later when some of his friends were sure to be there before going home to supper. McLeary would solemnly not let them out until Emmett Grogan had seen them.

It was fast getting dark and the night air settling down. Five steps Mr. Grogan took and sobered so suddenly it was like bumping into himself around a corner. He had better get home, he decided quickly. If he could make it, he added soon. With one block he was apprehensive, two and he was scared, three had him terrified. Something had him by the throat, no air was getting in, he was turning hot and cold, his joints were rusting fast. Holy Mary, Mother of God. Holy Mary, I'm not ready. His mind cleared long enough to wish this on his wife—take her, Lord, she's mean.

Mr. Grogan lurched up the steps of his house and found the door locked. It wasn't possible. Could she have gone out, thinking he might collapse? He fumbled in all his pockets at once, could not find his key, tried them systematically. No key. He wanted just to slump down on those stones and die crying. Maybe the back door was open, if only he could hold out that long. When finally he shoved it in she was sipping tea at the kitchen table and looked up as if she was seeing a ghost. That was when he really got scared. She was not shamming, probably never had been.

"Well, Mr. Big," she brogued, "I hope you enjoyed yourself."

"Oh," he managed to groan, leaning on the table edge, "sick. Terrible sick."

Mrs. Grogan drained her tea, picked a leaf off her tongue.

"Hah!" she snorted. "You? Grogan, the Iron Man? You've never been sick a day in your life. Told me so yourself many a time."

"Oh, I'm dying, woman. You were right. I admit it. I'm a sick man. A dying man. I admit it. Do you hear? What more do you want for your pleasure?"

"Get on with you, Grogan. Sober up. I've no time to be bothered with you."

Mr. Grogan licked his lips. They were hot and crinkly. "Will you just help me up the stairs a bit?" he whispered.

"Now don't let me have to tell you again, get out of my kitchen and leave me to my business. You're well enough to swill with the pigs at McLeary's, you're well enough to bring me up a scuttle of coal from the cellar."

Mr. Grogan turned and dragged himself out in an agony

of terror and pain. He crawled up the steps, pulling himself with rubbery hands, and into his room. He struggled out of his overcoat and shoes, laid his cap on the table and crawled under the covers as the phone began ringing.

"Hello," she said. "Who? Oh, Mr. Duffy, is it? Young Mr. Duffy," and she raised her voice to a shout. "Well, yes, he was a little under the weather earlier in the day, one of the same old complaints. No, no we didn't. I always just look after him myself. Serious? Well, you ought to know Grogan well enough for that. Bring yourself out on a night like this? For what? Why, he's just come in from McLeary's where he spent the whole afternoon. I'm surprised you didn't see him."

Quail for Mr. Forester

～～～～～～～～～～～～～～～～～～～～～～～～～～～～

W hether it was the same all over Texas I do
not know, but in Columbia there was quite
a rigid caste system based on the kind of goods a person
sold. To deal in notions was probably the lowest, and dry
goods was pretty low. Groceries was acceptable, pharmacy
quite acceptable, furniture almost genteel. In all this I
mean retail. To be in anything wholesale, even in a modest
way, was higher than to be in the highest retail. And yet
no kind of wholesale was higher than retail hardware. For
it was into that that the Foresters went, with that indiffer-
ence to the conventions which only they could afford,
when the last of the old family property was sold at public auction.

For a while after Mr. Forester bought the hardware store
it had looked possible that the town might bankrupt him
out of respect for him. No one could picture himself being
waited on by a Forester. The first customer told how it
seemed as if the world was coming to an end, and said
that she had had to turn her head while Mr. Forester
wrapped her package. Everyone had been touched and
pleased to hear that it had been a very clumsily wrapped
package.

But Mr. Forester had such dignity, and carried through with such an air of remaining untouched, that people grew to feel it was not too insulting of them to trade with him, and he began to show a profit.

It was not a very big store and certainly Mr. Forester did nothing to bring it up to date; people like the Foresters did not put on show. Yet in ten years, while the town, so to speak, turned its head in order not to see a Forester practicing economies, he saved enough to buy back—just in time for his wife to die there—his family home, the largest house on Silk Stocking Street. That was the nickname of the street, but to show you how generally it was called that, I do not even remember its real name. It was where all the quality lived.

We lived on Oak Street and every morning at eight o'clock Mr. Forester passed our house on his way to business. My mother would let the milk stay on the porch until it was time for him to pass, and he always tipped his bowler to her, and sometimes he paid her a compliment in the old style.

My father was a hunter, one who never came home empty-handed, and we never sat down to a dinner of wild duck or woodcock or quail but my mother thought of the faded sovereignty of the Foresters, of the days when none of their many tenants would have dreamed of a trip into town without bringing some fresh game for them. In the lull after I had said grace, while we spread our napkins, my mother was sure to say, "Wouldn't poor Mr. Forester enjoy some of this."

She would have sent my father to him with presents of fish and game, except that she was sure it would be a perfect waste, for though she had never set foot in the house, much less eaten there, my mother had decided that

Mr. Forester's Negro cook was not only a very poor cook, but that she took a vengeful delight in being so.

Time was, my father recalled, when hunters brought home towsacks full of quail, like to the present-day birds as a Brahma rooster to a bantam pullet; but when he and I, one fall Saturday in my twelfth year, brought home nine plump ones, we had had an unusual good day. When they were plucked and laid in a row my father said that, by Jim, you could almost recognize these as kin to the old-time quail. My mother seized this moment to suggest inviting Mr. Forester to dinner. Before she could take it back, my father said that that mess of birds was about as near worthy of a Forester as you would come nowadays, and, all right, we'd do it, by Jim.

He and I walked downtown. It was midafternoon and the square was filled with country folks. There were farm-wives in poke bonnets, with snuff stains at the corners of their mouths, and bold country girls in overlong dresses who would say even coarser things than their brothers whenever they passed a town boy like me. Ordinarily I hurried past, pretending an errand of deafening urgency, while I tried to fix my thoughts upon some moment out of history. It was thanks to these girls that I had some idea what the word *violation* meant and I was fond of imagining that I had only lately saved these unworthy girls from violation at the hands of Union soldiers, and of enjoying the irony of their ingratitude. Today I was glad to have my father with me. I was even gladder to have him guide me past the corners of the square, where the narrow-eyed, dirty-talking country men collected, squatting on alternate haunches all afternoon and senselessly whittling on cedar sticks until they were ankle-deep in curly, red-and-white, tobacco-spattered shavings.

A crowd was in the hardware store and both Mr. Forester and the Saturday clerk were busy. My father and I stood out of the crowd near the coil of hemp rope, and by breathing deeply of the dry, clean, grassy smell of it I felt purified and removed. I felt acutely what disgust must fill a man like Mr. Forester to have to sell cow salves and horse collars to such men, and to have to refuse to dicker with their women over the prices of pots and mops and over the measure of a dime's worth of garden seed.

The crowd thinned out and I strolled over to look at the showcase of pocket knives, but seeing the clerk heading my way I rejoined my father.

It pleased my father to be able to tell Mr. Forester that he had not come on business.

"No, sir, I have come on pleasure. Not that it is not always a pleasure, of course.

"This is my boy, Mr. Forester. Son, shake hands with Mr. Forester. He is a backward boy, sir, but do not take it to mean that he is not aware of the honor."

Mr. Forester's resemblance to General Beauregard added to the trouble I had remembering that he had not fought in the Civil War. At twelve, I had a very undeveloped sense of the distance of the past, and often, indeed, I found it quite impossible to believe that the Civil War was over. Certainly I could never believe that those remains of men, more like ancient women, who were reverently pointed out to me as Confederate veterans, could ever have been the men of the deeds with which my imagination was filled.

"Mr. Forester," said my father, "my wife has been after me I do not know how long to bring home some birds fit to ask company in to. Well, I went hunting today—me and the boy—and I will not say that what we brought home are fit, but as I said to my wife, I guess these birds are about as near worthy as I am ever going to come, for the birds do not get any better and neither do I."

I was aware of the solemnity of the moment by the lack of contractions in my father's speech.

"Now I would not know, myself," he continued, "but some say my wife is a pretty fair cook."

My father waited then, and in a moment Mr. Forester got the idea that somewhere politely concealed in that speech was an invitation to dinner.

Mr. Forester said, "Why now, this is mighty nice and thoughtful of you and your wife, John—of whose cooking I never would doubt. I don't mind saying that it has been a while since I had quail! Is it tonight that you want me to come? And what time would your wife like me to arrive?"

"What time do you generally take your supper?"

"Why, I generally take it around eight, but—"

"Then eight," said my father, "is when you shall have it tonight."

My mother suggested I be given my supper early and sent to bed. My father disagreed, as she had meant him to, saying that it was an evening I should want to remember, and that I was old enough to behave like a little gentleman now.

I was posted by the window to watch for him. Dusk spread in the street and it began to be dark. The street lamps came on at the corners of the block and I saw my friends come out of their houses up and down the street and gather in the light to play, and I wondered if they knew why I was not with them. I was hungry from the smells of the kitchen and restless in my Sunday clothes.

At last I saw him round the corner. He wore his bowler and carried a stick with which he lightly touched the ground about every third step he took. My friends in the light of the lamp watched him and when he was past turned to whisper among themselves, for some of them dared to think such people as Mr. Forester old-fashioned and amusing. He carried something cone-shaped and when he was halfway down the block I saw that it was flowers wrapped in paper.

At the door my mother took his coat and thanked him for the flowers and said she hoped he had not had too hard a day in the store. I was embarrassed at her mentioning that he had put in a working day, and using the word *store*, but my mother's sympathy for Mr. Forester was deeper than the town's, and went beyond any hopeless efforts to keep up appearances.

Mr. Forester turned from my father and extended his fist to me and opened it palm up. It held one of the knives I had seen in the showcase in his store. It was a pearl-handled knife, and as we went into the living room he said, "I thought you might like that one because I was very fond of one just like it when I was about your age. It was given to me by a Mr. J. B. Hood. Did you ever hear of him, son?"

I started to shake my head, then I thought and cried, "Do you mean *John Bell* Hood?"

"Sir," my mother reminded me.

"Oh, you know about John Bell Hood, do you?" said Mr. Forester.

My father guided him to a chair, saying, "Does he know about him! Sometimes I believe he thinks he *is* John Bell Hood."

"Well," said Mr. Forester, "he couldn't want to be a better man. Now could he?"

My mother excused herself to look after the birds. My father mixed drinks.

"Yes," said Mr. Forester, "John Bell Hood was often in our house when I was a lad. A great soldier and a great gentleman. *And* a cagey cotton buyer."

I laughed, but weakly, for I would rather he had not mentioned that last.

"You remember what General Lee said, son? 'In the tight places I always count on the Texans.' If they had had the sense to follow up Hood's victory at Chickamauga the South might have won the war."

"I can vouch for this mash, Mr. Forester," said my father. "I watched it made. It goes down like mother's milk."

Mr. Forester took a sip, held the glass to the light, cocked an eye appreciatively at my father, then for my benefit he put on a moral frown and, nodding the glass at me, said, "He was right about this stuff, too—John Bell Hood. You remember, when he was wounded at Chancellorsville they tried to make him take a drink of whisky to ease his pain, and he said he would rather endure the pain than break the promise he had made his mother never to touch a drop."

I felt my face redden and I stole a glance at my father.

"That was not John Bell Hood, sir," I said. "That was Jeb Stuart at Spotsylvania."

It was one of my favorite incidents.

"Was it?" said Mr. Forester.

"Yes, sir."

I looked at my father. He was glaring at me.

"It was Jeb Stuart," I said.

"The boy is probably right," said Mr. Forester. "It's a long time since I went to school—and you, too, John, for that matter. Whoever it was, it is a good story. And in any case it was a Southerner who said it. But I am glad to see that they still teach them about the war in school."

"Oh, school!" said my father. "He reads all that on his own. I will say that for him. If you depended on what they teach them at school—!"

My mother came in. We rose.

"The schools!" she cried. "You wouldn't believe it was Texas, Mr. Forester, the things they teach them in the schools nowadays!"

"Now, now," said Mr. Forester, "things can't have had time to change much since your own school days."

My mother turned red with pleasure. "Oh, Mr. Forester!" she cried. And she was so carried away she forgot what she had come in for and my father finally had to ask was she hatching those birds out there before she remembered with a cry, "Oh! That's it! It's served!"

The table had the leaf in. It was lighted by three tall slender candles in a triple-branched holder. The shadows on the silver and glasses were deep, and the highlights seemed thick, the way the white paint is laid on in old pictures. The water flask seemed filled with trembling quicksilver. Side dishes of black and green olives and pearl-like pickled onions were stationed around the center platter, in which, nested in fried potatoes as yellow and as slender as straw, were the golden-crusted quail. Nearby was a basket of smoking rolls blanketed with a white napkin. There were bowls of deviled eggs, brandied peaches, creamed onions, peas, mustard greens, whipped yams topped with toasted marshmallows, and a bowl of green salad shimmering with oil. Stacks of dishes stood waiting on the buffet and a bank of apples on a dish there glowed like dying coals. I could hardly believe I was in my own home.

When we had spread our napkins there was a silence and everyone looked at me. I bent my head, closed my eyes and said, "Bless us, O Lord, and these Thy gifts, which through Thy bounty we are about to receive through Christ our Lord. Amen."

"Amen," said Mr. Forester.

We were very hungry, for it was long past our usual suppertime. Mr. Forester was very hungry, too. So after everyone had servings of everything and Mr. Forester had praised each dish, for a few minutes there was no sound—not even the clatter of silver, since we were all mainly interested in the quail and this was eaten with the fingers—except, occasionally, the clink of a birdshot dropped on a plate.

When our first pangs had been assuaged my father signified the time for talk by leaning back in his chair, patting his stomach and looking gratefully at my mother.

"I seem," said Mr. Forester, "to recall having heard these birds disparaged earlier in the day."

"Well, you may thank old man Walter Bledsoe," said my father. "We got these birds in his oat field. It seems he gave up about halfway through this year, and left more oats standing than he took in to the barn."

Mr. Forester shook his head sadly.

"And to think," said my mother, "what the name Bledsoe once stood for."

"They have gone even further downhill," said my father. "Me and the boy were up to the house today to ask permission to hunt. You ought to have seen the place. Gate hanging loose, weeds grown up, junk in the yard—just one step away from white trash now."

"And I myself," said my mother, "remember when old Miss Jane Bledsoe thought nothing of going over to Europe every other year and bringing back a boxcar full of souvenirs and treasures."

"Even then," said my father, "she was spending money she didn't have."

"Well, in those days you didn't expect a woman like Miss Jane Bledsoe to keep up with whether or not she had it to spend," said my mother.

We returned to our food, this time talking as we ate.

My father said, "Getting back, Mr. Forester, to what you were saying earlier. About the South winning the war if they had followed up the victory at Chickamauga. It is interesting, isn't it, to try to imagine how things might be now if it had turned out the other way?" He laughed a little from embarrassment.

"Well, I can think of a few things that would be very different," said my mother with a meaningful, sad look at our guest.

"Yes, yes," said my father.

"People may laugh at us for fighting it all over time and time again—even Southerners, the kind coming up now—but they just don't know," said my mother.

"Not that *you* remember any much better times," said my father with a laugh to her.

"No," said my mother, "Lord knows that's true. But I've been told. Well, but it's not for *us* to tell *Mr. Forester*."

"Well now," said he, "I don't know. We have the electric lights now and the telephone, and now the automobile."

"Doubtful blessings," said my mother.

"And there is the motion picture," said Mr. Forester.

"Indeed there is," said my mother.

"Oh, I agree with you in disapproving them," said Mr. Forester, "as a general thing. But some of them, you know, are quite amusing, I must say. Very amusing," and he chuckled ever so softly over some memory.

"Light amusements," said my mother sternly, "don't seem becoming to people with what we have to remember. That's how it seems to me. Of course, you don't need any reminders, Mr. Forester. Not a person who has what you have to remember."

"Yes, our family lost a lot, of course," said Mr. Forester. "But then, every family with a lot or a little to lose lost it, and I am sure it was less hard on such as we than it was on those who may have lost less, but lost all they had."

There was a moment's silence.

"By Jim!" said my father. "Excuse me for being carried away, but that was well said, Mr. Forester!"

"Still, we don't have to be modest for you," said my mother. "And we know how much more it must have hurt the more you had to lose. Anyhow, it's not the money loss alone I mean. It's the whole way of life, as they say."

"Yes, yes," said Mr. Forester somewhat impatiently. "But times change and ways of life must change and we must accustom ourselves and make the best of it. Though I must say that this is the closest to the plentiful old way that I have been in a long while," and he indicated the table.

"Oh! Have more! Give Mr. Forester another one of those bird breasts. Here we have been talking and keeping him from the food!"

"Not at all. Not at all. You can see from my plate that nothing has been keeping me from the food! But I will just pick at another half of one of those birds."

With little urging he took a whole one, and he absorbed

himself in it so completely that my mother could watch him openly. As his enjoyment increased so did her sadness over the decay of the old South, as evidenced by Mr. Forester's appetite.

My father extended his plate and said, winking at me, "I vow, I believe I might work me up an appetite yet. Mr. Forester is ready for more, too. Give Mr. Forester that brown one there. That one was my best shot of the day—it must have been seventy-five yards, if I do say so myself."

"No more for me," said Mr. Forester. "I have disgraced myself quite enough already."

"Mr. Forester," said my mother, "you will hurt my feelings if you don't eat more than that little smidgin-bit."

"Well, ma'am," he replied, "I hope I am the son of my father enough not to hurt a lady's feelings," and he extended his plate.

"I just can't have any respect for a man with a finicky appetite," said my mother.

"Then you would have enjoyed making a meal for my father," said Mr. Forester. "There was a man who could eat!"

"We're none of us the men our fathers were," said my father.

The night had turned chilly and when we went into the living room after dinner my father lighted the gas stove. The gas lines had been laid in the town only that spring and the stove was a novelty still. It had pipe-clay chimneys and it was pretty to watch the red climb quickly up them from the row of sputtering blue flames. We had bought the stove at Forester's Hardware.

Mr. Forester said that they were just that week laying the pipes to bring the gas into his house. He would be glad to see the last of his sooty old furnace. It never had kept the big old house warm.

More and more, since his wife's passing, he said, as he watched the sputtering flames, he had thought of giving up the old place.

My mother said she hoped he did not mean that seriously.

Oh, said Mr. Forester, it would probably not come to anything more than talk. But something like we had, now —that would more than suit his needs, he, a lone man, without children—what use did he have for eighteen huge, high, drafty old rooms? The thing he could never understand was what had made him buy it back, how it was he hadn't known when he was well out of it. Probably simply because people expected it of him.

My mother said she supposed a certain amount of family feeling had been in it, too.

Mr. Forester said he supposed so.

My mother said she was sure of it, and that she did not think that it was a feeling to be ashamed of, surely.

No, of course not, said Mr. Forester. But when a person reached his age, for good or bad he began to think more of a little bodily comfort. Those old houses were all right in the days when people had big families and many guests always in the house, when relatives were closer than they were now and lived closer by and came often for long visits, and when people gave lots of parties and balls. But now—and what with the taxes . . .

"I declare it's a shame, just a shame," said my mother, "to make you pay taxes, Mr. Forester!"

Mr. Forester did not know whether this pleased him or not. "I don't understand," he said. "Why shouldn't I?"

"Taxes!" cried my mother. "On top of everything else!"

99

Mr. Forester colored.

"What short memories the people in this town have!" said my mother. "You might think that out of memory of old Colonel Forester and all he did for this town—you might think that just out of appreciation for your keeping up such a historic old home they might remit the taxes at least. What short memories! To me, Mr. Forester, you are a living reproach to them!"

Mr. Forester colored more deeply and turned to my father for help.

"Can't you just see them remitting the taxes!" said my father.

My mother shook her head sadly. But Mr. Forester laughed good-humoredly. He changed the subject. He and my father spoke of the cotton crop and of the coming state elections, while my mother got out her knitting and I sat listening, unnoticed. I was beginning to be disappointed in Mr. Forester. He did not seem different enough from us. And while I felt no particular shame of us, I did feel that Mr. Forester had lowered himself for the sake of his appetite to come to dinner at our house.

The clock on the mantel struck ten. Mr. Forester said it was time for him to be going. He was not good for much, he said, after ten o'clock on a Saturday evening.

Mr. Forester ducked his head to check a belch, then munched reminiscently a few times. He said he had not had such a dinner since—since he didn't know when. Since he was a boy. He ducked his head again, and when he looked up, his eyes, whether from gas or from emotion, were filled with tears.

"I can't tell you how much I enjoyed it," he said, first to my mother, then to all of us. "How nice it was of you to think of me and how—I—"

My mother was embarrassed and made a joke, saying he must come some evening when her cooking was really good.

Mr. Forester rose and we all followed him to the door. My father held his coat. When he had it on, Mr. Forester was overcome once more and again his eyes filled with tears.

"Really, I—" he began.

"It's only what you were brought up to expect!" my mother cried. "It's not as much as you ought to have every day! Don't thank us. The only thanks we deserve is for being among the few still about who realize that!"

Mr. Forester was taken aback. He smiled uncomfortably. He looked at my father and then at me. I could feel the tragic expression on my face, and the sight of my father's was enough to make me cry.

"It just makes my heart ache," said my mother.

My father gave a loud sigh. Mr. Forester slowly tapped his finger against the crown of his bowler. At last his face gave up the struggle, fell, and he, too, sighed deeply. I could stand it no longer, and I thrust his stick at him from the umbrella stand.

He bade us good night and we stood in the door watching until he passed through the light of the street lamp and into the darkness beyond. His stick, I noticed as he walked under the light, now touched the ground with each step.

My mother closed the door and she and my father turned. They became aware of me and stood looking at me. My father shook his head. My mother sighed her deepest sigh.

I felt that there was no hope for me in these mean times I had been born into.

101

Sister

∾∾∾∾∾∾∾∾∾∾∾∾∾∾∾∾∾∾∾∾∾∾∾∾∾∾

Sister came down to the kitchen very early to attend Queenie through her labor. She found the other cats squatting in the shadows, solemn and stiff, while Queenie held the center of the room. Each of Sister's cats was temperamental; Queenie, the oldest, was the most difficult. Sister was touched by her moans and stricken looks, but she reminded herself that Queenie did like to have an audience. What a fuss she made!

"Queenie, Queenie," Sister chided. But her voice was soft as a purr. In each of her cats what she loved was just the weakness in its character.

The other cats drifted to the door where some sat and some paced up and down, waiting to be let out. Sister comforted each in turn. "No, no. There is nothing you can do to help. But don't worry—Queenie is going to be all right."

She offered her warm milk, ground beef, a raw egg. But Queenie wanted only to lie in the sunroom, wrapped around herself, down behind the potted oleander.

Yet Sister felt she wanted company. She regretted scolding her yesterday for stealing Zee-Zee's chicken bone.

The whole house seemed to draw near to wait for Queenie's pains to begin. Without the rest of her cats,

103

Sister grew lonely and fretful. But she reminded herself of her responsibility. Queenie depended on her. Sister was always grateful for one more way in which she might be useful. It was gratitude—not pride—she felt in knowing that she could do more things than most girls of fourteen. She thought of her cousins Enid and Evaline and felt sorry for them; they missed so much enjoyment, being useless.

Queenie's labor soon began. Sister knew to keep away from her. The old cat clawed the floor; she grunted; she drew herself into a knot and rolled over and over on her back. With each of her spasms the fur stood up along her spine. Though Sister tried to sit still, before long she was biting her nails.

The first two kittens were each dark gray with darker stripes. But Sister soon found the ways to tell them apart. The third, which cried loudest, was paler. That one, like its mother, had a black ring around one eye.

"Well, that makes how many now?" asked Father as soon as he was told. His egg was boiling too long on the range, his toast burning, his coffee percolating too fast and his corn flakes getting soggy, while in the guest bathroom off the kitchen he was nicking himself right and left with the razor. Busy with Queenie, Sister had forgotten his breakfast until he was already downstairs. Now, hurrying to make it, she also had to mix food for the mob of impatient cats gathered under the kitchen window.

The food for her cats had to be just so, neither too hot nor too cold. It made a heavy panful, which she balanced on one hand while opening the door with the other, trying at the same time to keep the cats back with her foot. But, as usual, two or three slipped in, and unable to find their food, went scampering around the kitchen.

Sister divided the food fairly among six plates, gently holding off the cats.

Father smelled the toast burning and rushed from the bathroom, his face covered with lather which here and there was stained pink with blood. The stray cats scurried. There was a howl; he had stepped on one's tail. Exasperated, he dropped his arms. He wanted to curse but denied himself; he started to complain but words failed him.

He had managed to calm himself when he sat down to breakfast. Sister was especially quiet to keep from irritating him. She set things before him with the least commotion possible.

"How many does that make now?" he asked.

Sister busied herself at the sink and pretended she had not heard.

"Hmmm?"

She studied the tone of his voice; it did not seem reproachful. He smiled.

But he could not help shaking his head when Sister said, "Nineteen."

All he could do was make his old joke. "With all these cats, there soon won't be room for a mouse in this house."

Father pushed aside his corn flakes and reached for his eggcup. The smell he had been trying to ignore overcame him. Of all animals, cats smelled the worst! He laid his spoon down in disgust. He turned to say, "Good heavens, Sister! If you must keep them inside, can't you at least try to housebreak a few of them?" But as usual he found her gone without a sound.

The dog barked at a car coming up the drive. Walter looked at his watch. The kitchen clock was slow! Paul, his brother, came in, pleased to find him late. They took turns driving down to the train. On mornings when Walter was upset and cross, Paul took pains to be jovial and loud; let Walter try to feel good and Paul was surly all the way to the city. I do believe, Walter told himself now, that Paul enjoys coming in here and smelling this smell. To think of my having spent all the money I have on this place, only to have it smelled up like this by a pack of cats, must give him a great deal of pleasure. He knows it's a better house than his, and otherwise better kept. No doubt he thinks I haven't the nerve to set my foot down and put a stop to it, for he expects me to be intimidated by Sister as he is by Evaline.

Thinking like this would sometimes drive Walter to speak harshly to Sister. But usually he behaved, when Paul came, as though he smelled nothing, and would find a way of repeating what a pleasure it was to have many cats in the house.

No one else, Sister knew, felt about cats as she did. Someone might come to, though, someday, if she kept trying to make them see how nice cats are. Of those for whom she had hope, Uncle Paul seemed the most likely. Not because he already liked cats somewhat—he paid less attention to them than many people, in fact—but because he was the only person who often called her Jane, instead of Sister.

"Jane," he said, "what is that?" looking into the sun-room and peering at the box from which came cries and the sucking sounds of Queenie's kittens. Cocking an eye, he looked at Sister as though he had caught her doing something mischievous, but was prepared to be amused by it.

"Would you like to see them?" she asked. If only he would hold one and watch them feed, she was sure he would love cats forever.

106

Father said, "Sister, don't annoy Uncle Paul with your cats. Everyone is not like us, you know, when it comes to cats."

Sister was left standing. Uncle Paul had turned away, his interest lost.

Preceded by a loud yawn, Edmond sauntered in.

"Ah," said Walter. "Look who decided to get up."

"Dad," said Edmond, "you won't by any chance be near a bicycle shop today in the city, will you?"

"So," said Walter. "So that's what got you out of bed before I was gone." He lowered his eyes and said resignedly, "I might have known."

For one of Walter's great pleasures was pretending that Edmond had no feeling for him. Sighing and rolling his eyes at Paul to show how mistreated he was gave him intense satisfaction. Paul would give the world for a son to tyrannize him.

"What is it you need now?" Paul was asking. He too liked to make himself out a victim of Edmond's selfishness.

Looking from one to the other, Edmond could see that each would like to be the one to get a new tire for his bicycle. It was a good time to ask for a speedometer, too. He chose Uncle Paul, sure that Father would then buy both.

Paul looked at Walter to be sure he did not resent his intrusion. Walter smiled tolerantly. It warmed him to be able to let Paul sometimes feel himself the father of a son. Feeling warm, Walter shook his head in admonition, saying, "I don't know, Paul. I don't know. Keep this up and you will ruin him." Paul glowed. How he enjoyed being told he was making a fool of himself over that boy.

Walter had long ago imagined a scene that was bound to occur one day. Sooner or later Nancy, Paul's wife, was

107

going to burst out with all her resentment and say, "If that boy were mine—!"

And that was as far as she would get.

"My dear Nancy, that is just the point. He is not yours."

And with those words, Walter felt sure, he would be saying what Paul had wanted to say all these years.

Sister ducked her head and rubbed her eyes with the back of her hand. Father had got off. She had made Edmond's breakfast. The dishes were washed and replaced and the laundry ready for Mrs. Hansen. What was it she had not done? She had made her morning inspection of the garden and with great care reset two iris bulbs which the cats had dug up. Had there been something she was supposed to remind Father of?

It was in the morning when the house was still, and at night just before bed that this feeling came over her. She would think and think and not recall what it was, but grow more certain by the minute that it was something important she had forgotten to do, or something urgent that someone had said to be sure to remind him of.

She had no more time to worry over it. At eight o'clock she must begin cleaning up after the cats.

Her routine was to start in the dining room, just outside the right-hand kitchen door. There, under the table upon which the wines were ranged, was sure to be a mess. It was one of their favorite spots.

Certainly it was contrary of the cats not to use the sandbox. In four rooms newspapers had to be spread in every corner and collected once, often twice a day. Yet Sister could not think of punishing them. The training was so cruel. Poor things, they could not help themselves, and she had grown accustomed to it.

To get under the Swedish fireplace was a job, and that was where Huckleberry always went. No place suited Zee-Zee but under the teakwood table upon which the samovar sat. Pinky favored a spot behind the cabinet of blown glass, while Dots, his sister, had a place behind the pottery cabinet.

No one could tell Sister that all cats were alike!

"Naughty Bo-Bo," she said each day as she went to clean behind a certain copper urn, and, "Dreadful Yvonne," she murmured, crawling under the dining table.

And Clarabelle, Helen, Walter, Little Nell, Hildegarde and all the rest, as she went behind the scented geranium, the lacquered screen, the Franklin stove, the table with the Swedish bowl, her voice growing softer and her smile broader as she went.

"Oh, naughty Leopold, naughty, naughty Harriet," she said. "And Mr. Micawber!" she cried on seeing that a leg of the breakfast-room table was being used again to sharpen claws.

The cabinets filled high with glass and china and the rows of copper vessels glowed in the darkened room. Sister crawled across the patch of sunlight spreading through the French doors.

She finished, straightened herself and took a slow, thoughtful sniff. She believed it was all right. She walked through the dining room, pausing at the likely spots to test the air, warning herself that she must be critical. Being so accustomed to the smell, she could not trust herself to judge for other people's noses.

Poised on the doorsill, before she would step in, Mrs. Hansen, the cook, stood sniffing.

Only once had Mrs. Hansen arrived before Sister finished cleaning up after the cats. It was a revelation to her;

109

she was scandalized. She still grumbled about people with so much money, a child so spoiled that she had not one, but umpteen cats to mess wherever the urge took them all over a house costing more than her dead husband, sweating day after day on a railroad line, ever made in his life, plus the little she had earned since he passed away, and often she would throw in all that her three children were ever likely to make, for good measure.

One would think it was Mrs. Hansen who had to clean up after the cats. Indeed, she believed that she did, and told her children so, describing the task in revolting detail, to reproach them still further for their everlasting ingratitude.

Always late, Mrs. Hansen, instead of apologizing, gave Sister to feel she ought to be ashamed, making a poor widow woman with three children of her own to get breakfast for, come then to attend her family.

All forms of quiet aggravated Mrs. Hansen. It gave her the creeps, she complained. She jumped and gasped each time she turned to find Sister standing near. When Mrs. Hansen had no one to talk to at the top of her voice, she hummed as loud as she could.

Mrs. Hansen began her day with a good loud complaint. She could settle down to work only when she knew that her grievances were in ahead of everyone else's. "Well, here I am," she declared.

Outside, cats bounded up in alarm and slunk off out of range of Mrs. Hansen's voice.

How was she to break the news of Queenie's litter, Sister wondered. She did not feel apologetic about the new kittens; but if she seemed to be, perhaps Mrs. Hansen would give in with a smile and a shake of the head. She had seen

110

people pass off their whims and weaknesses in a way that made others humor them.

"Oh, dear," she sighed. "Queenie had a new litter this morning."

"Well, if it's got you worried," said Mrs. Hansen, "I can tell you just what to do. Now, we have cats at our house. But," she said, "there's cats—and then, there's cats." The water for her tea was boiling. She turned to set it off the light. "I'm glad to see you've realized that it was getting out of hand. Now, if you'd like, I'll just put them in a sack and on my way home as I'm driving over the bridge—"

Mrs. Hansen drew herself up, listening suspiciously. She had the feeling that she was talking with no one to hear her. She turned. The child was gone! What a creepy feeling that gave her.

Sister was dusting in the library. Out in the garden Leonard knelt, patiently untwining the runners of the strawberry plants. The old Negro's face gleamed in the sun; it was the color of eggplant. Sister watched him rise and greet her mother when she came upon him from around the hedge, the special smile she had for him already on her lips. Leonard's ways gave Martha Taylor much amusement; she imagined he disapproved of most everything she did; she walked in the garden in pajamas.

Leonard's quaint uprightness made him a character. Guests were charmed by Martha's anecdotes in which she did something frivolous, and Leonard extinguished her with his solemn scorn.

She suggested work for him, sure that once she was gone he would fall back to snipping runners from the strawberries, declaring to himself that he knew what needed doing.

111

Martha took a turn among the flower beds, kneeling here and there to pluck a weed. At the herb beds she lingered to enjoy the sunshine and the fresh air and the smell of sweet basil and tarragon. She glided over the cobblestones of the court, ran her fingers through the Dutchman's-pipe that hung over the dining-room door and went in.

"Good morning, Mrs. Hansen," she said. "Ah, there's my boy."

Edmond came forward for his hug. He was beginning to wish to have it some place other than in front of Mrs. Hansen.

"Tell Mother what you've been doing, Sweet."

"Nothing," he said, meaning, nothing wrong.

"Did you have your breakfast? Was it good?"

"It was all right. Well, I have to go now. I'm going down to Billy Morgan's."

"Did you finish that birdhouse you were building?"

"Long ago. It wasn't so good. I threw it away."

"Oh—too bad. But then why not build another?"

"I have to go down to Billy's. He's got a pair of guinea pigs."

"You have had guinea pigs. You were never interested in your own. Wouldn't you like to stay and help me in the garden?"

"I'd rather go down to Morgan's."

"Aunt Nancy is coming this afternoon. Perhaps she will bring something for you."

Edmond shrugged. He knew the sort of things Aunt Nancy brought.

"Well," said Martha, "I know a little boy with a birthday coming up soon."

His birthday was twenty-four days away. Already she had begun teasing him. She enjoyed making him guess what he was getting and where it was hidden. As the time neared she worked him into a frenzy of impatience. Then, as on the day before Christmas, at the last minute she would tell.

"Oh, well," he said, "I'm not expecting much this year. Besides, it's not the gift that counts."

She could interest him in nothing. He was determined to go. Martha yawned and rose.

"Where is Sister?" she asked.

"Here."

"Good heavens, child!" Martha cried.

Sister stared. What had she done now?

"The way you slink up on people! Just look what you've done to poor Mrs. Hansen!"

Sister began accounting for herself since getting up.

"I watered the plants, she said, "and dusted the library. I took out the trash and burned it and put some rugs out to sun."

"Did your father leave any message for me?" asked Martha.

Sister thought for a moment. "No." She hurried to tell the other things she had done this morning. "I scrubbed the bathtub."

"Are you sure?" Martha asked.

"Yes. Edmond left a ring."

"Who, me?"

"No, no, no," said Martha. "I mean, sure that Father left no message."

She had been sure; now she hesitated.

Martha sighed wearily. "Well, I just hope it was nothing important."

"I swept the back steps," said Sister hopefully.

Martha said that that was thoughtful of her.

Sister smiled her bashful smile. She blushed. She felt encouraged to tell that Queenie had had her kittens.

"How nice," Martha said.

Sister watched her closely. "Would you like to see them?"

"All right."

"They're in the sunroom," Sister said. "I put them in a box. They're behind a plant. There are three of them. One has a ring around its left eye, just like Queenie. I've already named them. But if you can think of better names . . ." Her words trailed off as she realized that Martha might be annoyed with so much chatter.

The kittens were asleep. Sister stroked Queenie. She was proud of her. Martha knelt and cautiously put out her hand. Queenie growled.

"Queenie!" Sister cried.

When the tips of Martha's fingers touched her head, Queenie snarled. Sister gave her a hard slap. Growling softly, Queenie drew back in bewilderment. Sister, too, was astonished at what she had done.

"Come back, Mother," she cried. "She won't do it again, I promise." But Martha was gone. "Oh, Queenie," Sister moaned. "Why did you have to do that—just when things were going well."

Queenie sulked; she refused to make up, and it seemed to Sister that she looked misunderstood. She considered Queenie's side of the affair. A cat, she reminded herself, can tell when a person is only pretending to like it.

"Hot, isn't it?"

"It is, miss," said Leonard, barely looking up. The thin gray fuzz on his head was like pocket lint.

"It's the humidity," Sister suggested.

114

"That's what they say."

Sister wished she could find something to say that others were not always saying. Leonard was known not to like to waste words on the same old things.

"Now, missy, if you'll just stand out of my light I can tell which is the weeds and which is the vegetables."

She started. She was dreadfully embarrassed.

After a short wait, Sister softly cleared her throat. Leonard went on carefully teasing out a clump of crab grass.

"My," she said, "there are a lot of them, aren't there— weeds, I mean." She meant to sympathize with him.

But he thought she was saying that he had neglected his job. "Where they's dirt," he said, "they is bound to be weeds."

"Do you have a very big garden of your own?"

Seeing that he must talk, Leonard drew off his gloves and brought his pipe out of his jumper pocket and fitted it in the one place where he had teeth strong enough to support it.

"My old woman raises us a few things," he said. He looked puzzled as to how that could interest anyone.

He made his living raising other people's gardens, yet his wife raised theirs. Sister was tickled. Leonard smiled, too. Then he straightened his smile, as though he had caught his lips doing something without his permission.

All the same, Sister believed he was in a good humor.

"Do you have chickens?" she asked.

They did, and ducks and one old gander.

"And a cow?"

She could not quite catch whether or not they had a cow.

But dogs they had. Three. And they had cats, she supposed? No? No, the last cat they had had got run over on the highway, it must be—oh, six, seven years ago.

Its name was Citronella. Or maybe he had that one confused with another that was a little bit lighter in shade.

And had they never had another since?

Never another. No'm.

Sister said she hoped that was not because they had lost their liking for cats.

Leonard stopped sucking on his pipe and looked at her out of the corner of one eye. Was she working her way around to trying to give him one of them measly kittens?

"Well, to tell you the truth," he said, "we ain't much on cats. Dogs, now . . ."

Sister assured him that she was fond of dogs, too. Many people who loved cats were not, but she was.

"Now if it was puppies you was trying to get shut of, why, that'd be something else again," said Leonard.

For a moment Sister did not understand. Then, "Oh, dear," she cried. "You thought I wanted to—" She could hardly think of it. "Why, I'd never give one of them away. Not for anything." And certainly not, she thought, to a man who had just said he did not like cats.

Leonard chuckled. "Well, miss, now I knew that was just what you'd say. I was just testing you. I knew you wouldn't part with one of your kittens. And to tell you the honest truth, I do like cats. Like 'em fine. Yes, indeed —cats."

Sister smiled faintly.

Leonard knocked out his pipe. When he turned from picking up his gloves he found her gone.

"I'm sure it's very good of you to say so, Nancy—but it's perfectly inedible. And soufflé, you know, is a dish that Mrs. Hansen is so good at ordinarily."

116

"No, no, Martha," Nancy Taylor said. "It's fine." And Enid and Evaline spoke up, "Yes, yes. It's fine. Really."

Their table was in the grape arbor. Shashlik was slowly doing to a turn over a charcoal brazier within Martha's reach. The juices simmered from the meat and fell on the coals with a sizzle and a puff of smoke. The smell of sweet basil and fresh earth drifted in from the garden. The day was warm and still. Cats slumbered on the rocks.

"You are kind, all of you," said Martha gratefully. "Poor Mrs. Hansen. She worked so hard on her soufflé, too— knowing you were coming. You can imagine how badly she felt. After what happened, she wanted to make another one, you know, though the poor woman could hardly get a grip on her nerves."

"After what happened?" said Evaline.

"She saw a dead mouse," said Edmond.

"Edmond. Dear. Not at the table," said Martha.

"She always spoils the dinner when she sees a dead mouse," said Edmond.

"Or a live one," said Martha. "Which is considerably more often."

It was true that Sister's cats were rather slack at mousing. She fed them too much, Martha said. Loving cats had not made Sister hate mice. She loved her cats all the more because they did not molest them.

Martha gave a toss of her head. "Madness!" she cried gaily. "Plumbing that never works, a horse no one can ride, a gardener who won't let you near your own garden—and a houseful of cats that won't catch mice. Where else but at the Walter Taylors'?"

"But really, Martha," said Nancy, "I find the soufflé . . ."

"What that poor woman must think about this fantastic

household!" cried Martha. "The stories she must tell in the village about the Taylors!—*us* Taylors, I mean," she added with a smile.

"Oh, Lord!" cried Nancy. "And our Mrs. Porter about *us* Taylors!"

Martha smiled down the table upon her sister-in-law. And that smile dealt with all attempts to match her singularity.

Being poached upon by nineteen cats who caught a mouse a year, was one of the most delightful of the Taylors' whimsicalities.

"Nineteen!" visitors exclaimed. They were answered by Martha's smile, bashful and guilty, a smile that said: I know it's a weakness in me, but isn't it an adorable weakness.

"Well, I'm afraid we shall simply have to call the soufflé a bad job," said Martha, and pushed hers away. So did the others, their appetites for it fairly gone by now.

"May I have some more, please?"

This came from the end of the table.

Everyone turned and found it was Sister. A queer child.

Martha took the skewer of meat from the brazier. Cats stirred, yawning and stretching, sniffing the air.

Serving the plates, Martha said, "I suppose Sister has told you that three more were born this morning."

"Why, no," exclaimed Nancy Taylor, turning to smile at Sister kindly.

Perhaps she might have asked to see them, had not Huckleberry's paws appeared just then over the edge of the table. He jumped and landed near Evaline. Sister leaped from her chair. But Martha was already lifting him by the scruff and putting him on the ground.

"Do sit down, child," she said. "I can lift a cat."

When it happened that a cat could not escape punishment, Sister tried always to be the first to reach him. If it must be done, she would rather do it herself. There was never a person who could congratulate a cat while apparently scolding it, as Sister could.

A silence fell on the table. To break it, Aunt Nancy said, "What have you been doing with yourself since we saw you last, Edmond?"

"Oh," said Edmond casually, "just running true to form." He loved to spring phrases on them like that. There was a large family stock of the funny things he had said, and he was always hoping to add to it.

"Poor Mrs. Hansen had not quite collected herself, it seems, by the time she got to the pudding," said Martha.

Roast for dinner was in the oven, and in the quiet, clean kitchen where the clock on the wall ticked contentedly, Mrs. Hansen sat at the table sucking her teeth. Before her was spread her tabloid. Her eyes were wide and her lips indignant as she read; she held her breath while fumbling for the page in the back section where her story was continued. When she finished it she had to sit back, breathing heavily, and pat her chest to soothe the outrage in her heart. She saw herself coming home from working late to support her three fatherless children on a cold night down a dark deserted street. Suddenly, out of the shadows a figure loomed, reeling drunkenly. It made a guttural sound. It was . . .

Queenie—prowling in from the sunroom.

Mrs. Hansen yelped. Little did those three children Mr. Hansen left her with appreciate all that she went through for their sakes.

119

Sister, coming down the hall, heard Mrs. Hansen's gasp, and having some idea what might have caused it, turned and stole off to the library. She curled up on the sofa and found her place in a book. But the windows were open; there was a breeze in the maple tree and the steady rasping of Leonard raking the gravel walks. Soon she was asleep.

"Sister," said Martha, "bring me a pincushion."

Evaline's party dress was almost finished. She stood with one arm raised for Martha to let out a seam.

"Can't you find one, Sister?" Martha called.

"Here's one, Aunt Martha," said Enid.

"Thank you, dear. Never mind, Sister."

"She isn't here, anyway," said Enid. "She went downstairs long ago."

Martha smiled. "Worried over her cats, I suppose."

"Nineteen," said Nancy Taylor.

Martha gave the dress a final tug, and settled back in her chair. The studio had been filling with gentle, late-afternoon light, and Martha was moved to think of her own gentleness, her patience. She let Sister keep nineteen disgusting cats, with never a thought for her lovely home.

"It is a lot, isn't it," she said. She was filled with wonder at herself. "But you wouldn't want me to make her give them up?" She sighed. "I suppose it's what any other woman would do."

"But, Aunt Martha," said Evaline, "don't they make you—" She broke off with a shudder.

Martha said, "Yes—I forget, don't I, that they are disgusting to many people. That's selfish of me, isn't it? I mean, to allow my child to offend others." She sighed and said, "Perhaps, my dear, you will understand better when

120

you are a mother yourself. You know what they say about a mother's love."

"There is more than one kind of blindness," said Nancy, her voice grown suddenly hard.

Martha did not like her tone. She found herself getting excited. She said, "Well, I'd like to know of another woman with a house as fine as mine who let nineteen cats simply ruin it to please a child."

"Or to please her conscience," said Nancy. But she had not been able to say it as loud as she had meant to. The whine of a cat, beginning low and growing to a howl, had hushed them all. Nancy gave a shudder. Enid came to her and sat on the arm of her chair. Nancy hugged her reassuringly. Evaline came, too, a little jealous perhaps.

"Why," said Martha with a little laugh, "it's hard to imagine Sister without her cats."

They all sat trying to do it.

Dusk was turning to darkness. In the garden, under the balconies, among the plants in the rocks, cats were waking, yawning and stretching. They prowled in from the woods, from the drive, from the stables. One cat licked the table in the grape arbor, growling at all comers, while another searched beneath the table, sniffing for scraps.

They gathered in the courtyard. They perched themselves on benches, on tables, in the dirt of potted plants. One old cat found a vase in his way, knocked it off the table and settled himself comfortably. They all sat waiting intently, each securely in possession of his spot.

Sister yawned and rubbed the sleep from her eyes and raised herself to her feet with a mighty stretch.

She made her way down the dark hall, stepping over a pail someone had left in the way. Passing the windows, she could see the cats listening to her approach and gathering in the moonlight near the door, purring all together.

Sister held the door open. Huckleberry was the first one in, and Sister, with a smile and a nod, watched him make straight for his spot under the Swedish fireplace.

Man with a Family

I

She lifted the lid and peered in the churn to see if the butter had come. Straightening, she saw him round the corner, carrying one of his hands in the other as if he were afraid of spilling it. She dropped the dasher and ran to the door. He thrust out his hands as if she might know what to do with them. She reached for them, then drew back sharply and stood watching the blood fall on the doorsill. What was it now? As bad as the other times? He licked his lips, shook his head, then took his hand over and laid it on the table as if he meant to leave it there while he looked for something to patch it with.

From the range she brought a kettle of water and filled the washpan, testing it with her finger. As the blood swirled sluggishly through the water she sat tensely, brushing a wisp of hair back into her bun, wishing he would say something. She sighed and went to the bedroom and took a tattered pillowslip from the cedar chest. She bit a start in the cloth and rent it into bandage.

"Well," he sighed, "it was like this."

She sat down and turned her face up attentively, trying to look as she did when he told some favorite story, as if she had never heard it before, as if this was the first accident he ever had.

"I was plowing." He waited a second until she had him placed. He held his hands out, gripping the handles. She had it—there's Daisy, here's you and those are the reins around your neck.

"There was a big stone," he said, looking at the floor. She looked down at it with a frown. "But I didn't see it because it was covered. Now who would have thought of a stone in that south twenty?" he wanted to know, bristling a little, giving her a defiant look. She tried to show it was the last thing on earth that would have occurred to her. "In three years I never took more than a bucketful of stones out of that field. And they was all no bigger than your fist." She made a fist and laid it on the table; she honestly wanted to help him. "Smack!" he cried, trying desperately to steady the handles and straining his neck against the reins. She reached out to catch him and he caught himself a moment to remind her that she was at home churning butter, so she settled back and helplessly watched him flung over the handle bar, shoot out a hand to catch himself and rip it to the bone on the moldboard.

The story finished, Dan snorted, looking around him for some explanation, some reason for it, and she looked, too, glaring blamefully at the air around her. The story finished, Laura roused herself and realized suddenly that he would never get the cotton planted.

As he held out his hand for her to wrap Dan said apologetically, "I figure it was that last heavy frost pushed that stone up so high."

"I suppose," Laura sighed.

He gave a laugh to show how little his fault it was.

"What is it to laugh about?" she demanded.

They talked about other things driving home from the doctor's office but Laura couldn't help being a little suspicious. Surely he had been more careless than he admitted. In this past winter he had cut one thumb, twisted his knee, broken a rib, sprained an ankle and got a sliver of steel in his eye. To recall all that, why, who wouldn't be suspicious, and who wouldn't be aggravated with him? Of course he didn't do any of it on purpose and of course he was the one that suffered. When it reached the point where she just had to speak her mind about it, naturally she was not mad at him. But somebody had to insist he be more careful. She took her eyes from the road, trying to harden herself to speak plainly. Then she saw what he was hoping she wouldn't see, how much pain his hand was giving him and how carefully he was coddling it. She mumbled something about putting it inside his shirt and though he had heard her, he looked at the gasoline gauge and said he thought there was enough to get them home.

At four o'clock the school bus settled with a crunch before the gate and Harold came stamping in, yelling back from the door to friends and, without looking, flung his books on the table with a splash.

"What's he doing home?" He jerked a thumb toward Dan as he rifled the breadbox.

"He cut his hand," said Laura in a shooshing tone, trying to look a little respect into him.

He wanted to see. Laura said it might get infected. She added impressively, "It's got stitches."

"Stitches!" He gave Dan a look of respect. "Did it hurt much?" he asked.

"Lord, of course it hurt, silly!" Laura cried. "What do you think?"

He wanted to know how he did it.

125

"Oh," said Dan, "plowing. Hit a stone and fell against the moldboard." It sounded a little silly to tell it now and Harold looked as if he thought it did, too. "A big stone," he added.

"Why didn't you hold onto the handles?"

"What do you think I was doing, dancing a jig?"

"Here," said Laura. "Now you leave him alone. You go on out and play."

Harold drifted to the door and then wandered back. Coming close to Laura he said low, "You mean he's had another *accident?*"

There was rain every day for a week. Dan mended harness and puttered impatiently around the chicken yard. But rain could not have come at a better time, so he was not too downhearted. Laura was glad to have him home once she got used to the idea. She enjoyed shooing him out of the kitchen and showing him how to make fudge that always turned to sugar and had to be given to Daisy and reading the serial in the back numbers of the *Country Gentleman* aloud to him in the afternoons.

She finished milking on the third morning while he stood awkwardly by, then he grabbed the pail to take it to the house, took three steps and a corncob rolled under his foot, twisted his ankle and turned him end up in a puddle of milk. It was so funny they both rolled on the ground laughing but when he tried to get up she had to help him. But that was funny, too, and as she wrapped it up she said that pretty soon he would look like he had been hit by a truck and would need somebody to lead him around. He hobbled like an old, old man, but when Harold came home it would have been hard to tell he was limping even a little if she had not known it already.

126

Catching Harold's eyes on him, Dan decided to see what he could do with one hand about that old stump at the corner of the chicken yard that he had let stay there so long. He went over to it and spat on his hand, gave it a careless tug, then a heave, then nearly broke his back on it but it wouldn't budge. He looked around and decided to move that big stone he had let lay there for years, gave it a yank and it came loose. He raised it 'way above his head and threw it over the fence, then went casually back for his jumper, but Harold was gone. He looked back at it and had to admit it was not such a big stone at that.

II

Anxious as she was to have him get back, it did seem foolish for a man to think of planting cotton when his wife had to harness the mule. She was about ready to go to the field with him. Thank heaven, at least they were not that bad off yet, for the neighbors to see her walking behind a plow.

In low places in the fields, Laura thought, the ground would still be muddy. Neighbors who could afford to would stay home another couple of days; she hoped Dan didn't feel she was rushing him. She snapped the trace chains and settled Daisy's collar better. Dan gripped the handles and smiled at her.

As innocently as possible she said, "Now be careful, Dan," and he replied without resentment, "I will."

Laura might have canned a lot more peas but for looking up between every two she shelled, expecting to see him coming in with a limp or a drag or a stagger. Now that he had already lost so much time she feared he might be overcautious. Like Harold—leave him alone and he brought

127

the milk in without spilling a drop, but just let him spill it once and then tell him to be careful not to, how much it cost and all, and he stumbled with it sure as the world.

A drummer came to the door and usually she simply couldn't turn one away, but today, as this one rounded the corner, she kicked over her bucket of pods, scared stiff, and almost slammed the door right in his face, he had given her such a scare. As the day passed she got jumpier. It was silly, she knew, but to think of any more delay in the planting made her run cold all over. Maybe she imagined it, but Harold looked around the place as if it surprised him, too, not to find Dan home with some ailment or other. She sent him out but he moped around the back door. Dan was late and to get Harold to bed and give herself something to do she gave him his supper early. He ate slowly while Laura fretted whether she ought to cook a supper of Dan's favorite things, or would that seem she was making an occasion of a day that ought to be passed over as nothing out of the ordinary?

Harold finished and went to the window. It was dark now and he sighed lumpily, "I wonder what happened?" Laura turned to snap something, but he was already in the bedroom and instead she sat down to cry when she heard Dan's step. If he noticed her red eyes he never let on and probably he didn't; he was blind tired. His arm was stiff and she guessed he had followed the plow bent double all day, one handle in the crotch of his arm to spare his hand.

As he got back into shape he came in less tired, able to sit up after supper and read a while, or try to read but not be able for watching Laura, seeing how worried she had been all day and how, through the evening, she tried to accustom herself to the notion that another day had been got past, able to see that something, something he couldn't just put his finger on, but something peculiar had settled down in his house, and what was even more peculiar, even harder to find words to suit, something that seemed to mean to stay. He felt left out of everything. It was as if he had gone away for a while and come back before he was expected. It was such a queer feeling and it wasn't helped any by looking up sometimes and seeing Laura and Harold standing together like a photograph he hadn't got into.

The way they looked at him! Like they had really had something different in mind, but he had come and they had used him and now they couldn't send him back. Did they? Maybe he imagined it; he wasn't feeling good, anyway. Maybe his mind was all tired and bent over, too. But what could you think when your own boy looked at you like a horse somebody was trying to sell too cheap, and when he went to bed was thirstier than ever before and kept having to go to the pot to see if you had managed to keep on your feet once you had him out of sight?

III

Laura's mama came over as soon as she sent word that the washing machine had come. It was Saturday and Dan had gone into town to buy groceries, but Harold was too interested in the machine to go with him. Laura's mama drove her buggy over early. She loved machinery and was proud of her daughter for owning the shiny, mysterious washing machine and being able to run it. She loved the noise and loved having to yell above it to make herself heard.

"You might get that thing to churn butter," she urged in a shout.

Harold was disgusted but Laura thought it might work and promised herself to try it. Now the grandmother wanted to shut it off and give it a rest and rest herself. She rubbed a finger over it as tenderly as over a sleeping baby.

"A thing like that must cost a heap of money," she said.

Laura swelled with pride. "I should think it does."

Her mama stood with her question on her face but the amount was almost too much for Laura to be proud of. She said, "We bought it on the installment plan, of course."

"Well," said her mama, as though she had been taken for some kind of a fool, as though she didn't know a fine piece of machinery when she saw it, "I never thought you could buy such a thing outright," and in fact she couldn't really see how they had made the down payment. "How much was it?" she asked hungrily and cocked her ear around to receive some astounding figure.

She looked ready not to resent the price but to admire it. Laura couldn't think of another woman anywhere around whose husband had spent so much money on her at one time, so she told. Her mother flinched as if somebody had suddenly blown in her ear. She had prepared herself for the limit; now her face turned sour and she looked at the washing machine with distaste. She thought she had raised a more sensible daughter and one not nearly so trifling. She had washed work-clothes and dirty diapers on her seventy-nine-cent washboard for forty-odd years and it was good enough for anybody. She began to take notice that Laura's dress had a hole under the arm and that Harold had on pants too small for him and needed a haircut. Well, she never thought she would see the day when Laura would let her family go to seed and put her man in debt for years because she was too lazy to wash his clothes, and she said as much.

Laura said, "Well, I don't know as it will keep him in debt all that long."

"However long it is, looks like you'll sure be ragged but clean."

"Well," said Laura, standing sharp, hands on her hips, "if I am it'll be no change from what I always was at home. Except maybe cleaner," and she turned the machine on with a clatter and stuffed it with practically every stitch the family owned.

Grandmother recalled the bag of candy she had brought and fished it out of her purse. She took one herself and called Harold over and gave him one.

Laura snapped off the washer and said, "Don't feed him that junk this near dinnertime."

"Let him have it," Grandmother insisted, and with a look at the washer, "I don't suppose he got much while you was saving up for that thing."

"I declare, Mama, I never thought I'd see the day," said Laura, "when you'd envy your own daughter a little comfort and not like to see her come up in life."

"Comfort," said her mama, "is for them as can afford it."

"Well, you just let me worry about affording it. And this is only the first. I mean to have a lot of nice things and I'm looking around now to decide what I'll get when the crop's in."

"Yes, I've seen a new player piano," her mama sighed, "and a new second-hand car come to our house and seen the men come and take them away when they was half paid for." She shot the bag of candy at the boy; it was giving her a toothache. "Probably the last you'll see for some time," she mumbled.

Harold looked at his mother to have this denied.

Laura snapped at him, "I reckon you get enough candy."

"I don't either," he appealed to his Granny. "I've never got enough candy in my whole life."

Laura sent him out the door and no buts about it. The old woman called after him, "You just come over to your Granny's. She's always got a little candy for her boy.

"You better send that thing back," she said. She was serious now. "You never know what's going to happen to keep it from getting paid for."

"You're just mad," said Laura, "that Dan wants me to have a few nice things when Papa never bought anything nice for you."

"Never mind that kind of talk. You just better get rid of it." She clamped her bonnet on and gave the washing machine a scampering look.

"I was going to say you could bring your wash over and use my new machine," said Laura, "and to show you how big I can be, you still can."

Her mama replied with a lift of her nose to show that she wouldn't be caught dead doing it, "No, thank you. Thank you just the same. I've come this far without it and I reckon my rub-board will see me the rest of my way. You as much as said I keep a dirty house. Besides we ain't got as much clothes as all that," and she gave Laura's wash-pile a look that said as plain as day: But it's a good deal more than you all have.

IV

When the cotton was in the ground they all drew a deep breath. He was only a week or so behind with it, and then he started seeding his corn. That went so well that Dan spoke of taking off to go fishing. Laura looked forward to it and had it on her mind as she carried whey to the chickens. What a pity Harold was in school, she was thinking, when Dan came over the hill on Daisy.

Laura poured the whey in the trough and went out to meet him. He looked disgusted with something, so the fishing trip fizzled out.

"What happened?" she asked, holding the reins. Then she stooped under the mule's neck and she saw where Dan's leg dangled down and floated stiffly inside his bloody pants. Just above the knee his leg took a sickening jump to one side, like a pencil seen through a glass of water.

Laura crept out from under Daisy's head and started to look up, when she fainted. Dan slid off Daisy and got his good leg under him. But there he was stuck. He thought, Daisy might take it into her head any minute to make off for oats in the barn. Then what would he do? The nearest support was a fence post he could never reach. He couldn't possibly get on her back again. How long would she stand still? How long would it take Laura to come to? How long could he stand the sun without keeling over?

"Laura!" he shouted and Daisy shied. He licked the sweat from the corner of his mouth and called her more softly. Hanging around Daisy's neck, he inched his good leg out and gave her a shove, waited a second and when she didn't stir he kicked her. Laura, with a groan, rolled over and buried her face in the dirt. Dan could feel himself going and decided it would probably be best to fall a little to his left and forward.

Laura got propped on her elbows and shook herself down and got to her feet. Dan moaned as she tried to raise him. Maybe moving him would make things worse. She looked around, half-expecting someone to see the trouble

she was having and come over to give her a hand. She went
to the house and got a quilt. She wrapped him in it and
started for the car to go to the neighbor's phone.

Laura's papa sat at the table and steadily cropped the
shreds of his cigarette, his coffee saucered and blowed,
being careful to swill it quietly, stiffly respectful, which
consisted in not hearing anything that was said to him and
looking as if, under the circumstances, words just didn't
reach him, trying to keep his own two good legs out of
sight and not look any too well himself. Laura's mama
worked quietly over the stove and Harold sat in the corner
he had hardly left all day, trying to make himself as small
as possible, scared to death. He would not go into Dan's
room and Laura didn't insist. The sight of him could only
have made Dan feel worse.

Laura pulled her hands out of the bucket of plaster and
scrubbed them thoughtfully in the washpan. She picked
up the heavy bucket and her papa looked like he would
offer to carry it but he had had his own reverses lately and
too much must not be expected of him. He rubbed a hand
along a tender kidney and looked wistfully away.

The doctor plastered the leg. "Well," he said, "we might
have waited till a little more of the swelling went down,
but I don't think it will matter too much."

It didn't matter much to Dan. He looked at the leg
with only the top layer of his eyes. He brought himself up
with a bitter sigh and said, "He says I'll be in bed six
weeks," and gave Laura a long defiant stare.

She had already told herself it would be a long time but
now her surprise showed and so did her pain. Dan's tone
hurt her. He didn't have to throw it up to her like that.
She hadn't asked.

"That at least," the doctor said. "What I said in fact was six to ten weeks." He gathered up his tools and laid them neatly in his bag, taking out a bottle of pills. "Give him these to sleep but never more than three a day. I'll come out every day for a week or so. I don't know just what time of day but I'll get here."

"What I don't know," said Dan, "is when you're going to get paid."

"Well, I'll worry about that."

Out in the kitchen the doctor washed his hands, rolled down his sleeves and drew on his coat while everyone watched. Laura's papa nodded sagely at his movements and her mama stopped setting the table to pat her hair in shape and smooth the ruffles of her dress.

"I wouldn't leave him too much alone," said the doctor. "Keep his mind occupied. Just don't make too much over it. Course you can't exactly act like nothing happened," he smiled broadly, "but remember, it could have been worse."

How? How could it have been any worse, Laura wanted to know. He said that to everybody without thinking. Her papa registered with a snort that he thought it was bad enough.

The doctor settled his things in his pocket and turned to the old man. "Well, John, how've you been coming along lately?"

It was no time to feel well when a doctor was talking to you free, so the old man dug out his cigarette and got ready to give details. "Well, when you get my age, you know, Doctor, ever' little thing—"

The doctor pulled up his watch and glanced at it impatiently. He has other calls to make, thought Laura with some surprise, other bones to set. She got a glimpse of her papa rubbing up his rheumatic knee as though to polish it for show. She saw the fright in Harold's eyes over all these broken bones and aching knees and cut hands. She saw her mother reach over and set the turnips aside to simmer and look at the doctor as though she would like to ask him to stay for a bite but was ashamed of what her daughter had to offer.

Laura slammed the door and buried her face in Dan's arm. He let her cry and then raised her to him. She hugged him and sobbed. He stroked her head gently and gently eased her back a little. She had shaken him and the pain in his leg was awful.

V

Mr. Johnson hung soggily on the barnyard fence while Dan stood stiff and uneasy before him, not knowing what to do with his hands that he was keeping respectfully out of his pockets. Not far away Mr. Johnson's car rested in the shade of a tree, with Mr. Johnson's wife in the front seat. Mr. Johnson took out his cigar, shot a stream of juice onto a flat stone and watched it sizzle.

"I ain't been mean, have I, Dan?"

"No, Mr. Johnson," Dan replied, "you been mighty patient and I appreciate it. But, Mr. Johnson . . ."

"Now, Dan," he interrupted, "you know as well as I do, not many men would have strung along with you as far as I have."

"I know it, Mr. Johnson. You been mighty patient."

"Well, these things just happen. I reckon everybody has a stretch like this some time or other." Mr. Johnson waved a large chunk of charity at him. "I don't want to be mean. I ain't forgot you done well here before all this begun to happen. I don't forget them things. But now, you see, prices is good. This here's a good piece of land and with proper work we'd have us a whopping big crop off of it. Everybody else is doing good this year. You got one of the best sixty acres in the county right here, Dan, and you and me could both be making a killing if it was going right."

Mr. Johnson removed his big lazy Panama and mopped his forehead and the back of his neck with a sopping handkerchief. Dan shifted the weight from his aching leg slowly, trying not to wince. What was the good of all this? Why stand out here in the sun and jaw about it? He hadn't done it on purpose, for God's sake. Didn't he know it was a good year, and who stood to lose the most, him or Johnson?

"You've got a good head on you, Dan," Mr. Johnson was saying. "You ain't wild. You're about as settled a man for your age as I ever seen. I knew your papa and I could see his boy would make a good farmer. I just mean to say I got faith in you, Dan. But you can see the fix this puts me in."

Dan nodded wearily and followed Mr. Johnson's eyes down along the length of his stiff leg.

"Jesus, it ain't your fault. But it ain't mine, either." Mr. Johnson was getting hotter and his eye acknowledged an impatient stir from his wife.

"Well, I don't know what to say. We'll just have to let things go on like this for a while, I guess. I don't see nothing else we can do."

Neither did Dan. He stood helplessly, wishing Mr. Johnson would go on and not stop at those awkward spots.

"I can bring in a team and make another alfalfa cutting. And we might get a stand of soybeans if the weather holds.

But if anything else happens, God help us. Dan, you just got to be more careful."

Careful! It made him so mad he heard the insides of his ears pop. Careful! He raised his head, raised a forefinger, raised his leg to set it out before him in a stance, then thanked the Lord for the pain it caused him. Johnson would never know how near he had come to a good round cussing.

Mr. Johnson turned to go. Reaching into his pocket he brought up a lighter for his guttering cigar. At a gesture Dan went closer. Mr. Johnson, with a show of lighting his cigar, slipped a bill into his hand and signaled his wife that he was coming, that only the lighting of his cigar was keeping him.

VI

When Harold's summer vacation began Laura bent over backwards being nice to him. He'd been through so much, poor little fellow, had taken Dan's accident so serious and she had scrimped him on so many things he needed. Most of all she was ashamed of being sorry to have him home. She even refused to call him down when she knew he was bothering Dan with his racket. And Dan was being so nice, even softened her when once or twice she did fly off the handle at the boy.

Dan felt that his accident had done one good thing at least, brought him and Laura closer together than they had been since they were married, certainly a lot closer than they had been for a long time lately.

Not that he wasn't worried just about every minute. He worried over the look of things, what the neighbors were saying about Laura spading the vegetable garden and pitching manure out of the barn. They had seen her, all right, gone out of their ways to see her and he worried most over how she felt about the loss of her pride.

One Saturday after she had gone to town he found the washing machine gone. How she managed to get it into the car by herself he couldn't guess and didn't ask. Someday he would get her another one, meanwhile it wasn't as if it was any comedown. It wouldn't hurt her to wash a few clothes.

Laura said, "How did you do it?" glaring down at the boy. She was worn out with chopping kindling and he had been going like a wild Indian since the break of day. She would have to leave off her cooking and trying to get in a few strokes on the churn and trying to clean up the place that had got to looking like a pigsty and having to move Dan around to sweep under his feet with him sitting there like he didn't even know she was in the same room, much less trying to clean up where he was, have to break off and leave things to boil over and burn and come out to drag Harold down out of the mulberry tree or off the barn roof or out from under the house where all kinds of spiders and snakes were liable to get at him, a dozen times she'd had to come out and yell at him for something and now this cut thumb was the last straw.

"Drawing the knife towards, you, I bet, weren't you?" He made her mad the way he stood there so hangdog and she had a mind to grab him and shake a little of the nonsense out of him. Didn't she have enough to do without this now and didn't anybody care even enough to look after their own selves? "How many times have I told you never to whittle towards yourself? Huh? How many times? Well, just march over to that washpan and daub it good with iodine."

He twisted his face up at her with a plea. "Couldn't I use monkey-blood just as good?"

Dan put his paper down with a rustle and the boy looked at him with a slow flush of accusation, his eyes coming to rest on the leg stretched out under the table. He turned to Laura and began to whimper. She snatched him a turn and gave him a little whack, warmed up to it and gave him another.

"Stop it," said Dan. "He wasn't doing that a bit. I saw him and he was cutting away from him."

Laura shut her arm off midway and turned the boy to face her. He turned himself back and stared at Dan in bewilderment. Dan ducked back into his paper and when Laura looked down at Harold she knew instantly it was a lie. But what should she do? Not ask him and have Dan shown up, or if he said it was so, why, she'd be just encouraging him to lie. He started to tremble and she knew he was thinking the same thing. Poor little fellow, what a fix to put him in. He shied away when she tried to hug him. Dan put his paper down and cleared his throat and limped to the door while they both stood and gaped at him. The thought in Laura's mind scared her and made her ashamed. Her husband, the father of her child, and for a minute she had stood there and just hated him.

Harold knew how bad he always got to feeling after he told a fib, so he thought Dan might use a little cheering up. He found him in the barn and said, "You know, that was a pretty deep cut I got," thinking he would give him a little company.

"It didn't look like much to me," said Dan.

"Yes, it was but I didn't cry a bit."

"Why should you have? It wasn't nothing but a scratch."

Harold thought deeply. "I'm not as big as you are and for my size it was just about as much as your cut hand was for you." After a moment he added gravely, "I don't think it needs stitches, though."

"You look like stitches," said Dan. "You couldn't even stand the thought of a little iodine."

"Do you think I ought to lay off with it for a few days?" asked Harold.

Why, the little smart aleck! Dan drew back his hand to fetch him a good one, then let it fall. "Get out of here," he said, "and leave me alone. And the next time I catch you whittling towards you I'll give you such a whipping as you never had."

VII

Dan had been on his feet about two weeks when Mr. Johnson brought over a riding plow and an extra mule. Dan could not really make out now, he knew it and had for a long time, but maybe he could keep from getting quite so far in the hole with some late-maturing truck crop. He had the land for it, three acres, black as coal.

"Now, Dan," Laura pumped herself up to begin, "I hope they won't be nothing else happen. And probably nothing will." Lord, what else could? "But you never can tell and it's better to be safe than sorry. I was thinking, what if something was to happen and you wasn't able to get home. Here you are now still in that cast, I mean, and so you ought to have some way of calling me. Just in case, you understand."

Dan nodded. He couldn't afford to seem mulish.

She looked at him to see if it was all right to go on. "Now

they's an old cowbell hangs in the barn. Suppose we wrapped up the clapper and hung it on your plow, then, just in case—"

She stopped. He was hopping mad.

It made him madder every time he thought about it all day long and he wouldn't have spoken a word to her when he came home if he hadn't come with a big blue bruise like a windfallen plum over one eye where he had fallen off the plow seat and just laid there, unable to believe it, for half an hour. So he spoke just about a word and Laura didn't urge him to any more. Herself, she hadn't one. Next morning, without letting her see, he took the big brass cowbell off its hook in the barn, wrapped the clapper in a strip of burlap and hung it under the plow seat. It made him feel like a fool, like a clabber-headed heifer that jumped fences, but when he reached down to yank the thing off and throw it in a ditch the blood pounded in the knot over his eye and he left it.

He plowed along and tried to forget it was there, but it might just as well have been strung around his neck. He couldn't be mad at her, she meant well and he was past pretending she didn't have reason for fear. He had got to feeling like he ought to have a bell, not to call anybody to him, but to warn them he was coming and they'd all better hide so they wouldn't catch whatever it was he had. People already looked at him like they would rather he didn't come too close, like he had caught something nasty, not to be spoken of. He didn't imagine it, no more than he imagined the look on Mr. Johnson's face the last time he was over, like he just couldn't see how a man could change overnight and go so completely to the dogs, shaking his head as much as to say, I don't see how you could do it, a man with a wife and family. Then again, half-awake in the morning, aching all over and dreading the clang of the alarm, he would see a long row of backs all turned his way and hear sniggers, "You know, he ain't no good to his wife any more. Ain't been for months. So just keep your eye on her for the next little spell."

He knew people talked about how tacky he dressed them, too, her and Harold. It looked like every dress she owned had a way of coming out at the seams under the arms and though he knew she had a lot to do, it did seem she could keep her things mended a little better. Not that she left those holes there to make him feel bad, but she ought to have seen they did.

Then her mama and papa would come over and the old woman would sit with her nose stiff and her eyes loose, looking behind and under and atop things as if what she saw before her, bad as it was, wasn't bad enough, and she was sure they had worse things hid away. And the old man would sit and rub his belly, ducking his head, pumping up a good long belch that rumbled like an indoor toilet, letting everybody know what a good dinner he had left home on and how little he looked forward to getting here for his supper.

The old man was the only one didn't think he had a nasty case of something. He just thought he was lazy and he had a sly steady look for him: I know what you're up to, tried it myself, but hell, they's a point to stop at and you passed it long ago.

And now, even Daisy, turning round with a long disappointed look at him. He pulled the team up, thinking he would eat, but he couldn't get a bite down.

He thought how Laura's mama shook her head over Harold every time she laid eyes on him. Dan couldn't see anything wrong with him. Kids were supposed to be a little dirty and wear old clothes around home. But to her he was such a pitiful sight, maybe he was just closing his eyes to all that was wrong with the boy.

He thought how long he had let that twenty-dollar bill Mr. Johnson slipped him stay in the cupboard, how he vowed to go over and give it right back the very next day but hadn't got around to it somehow, and instead come to say he'd let it lay there and never use it and return the very same one when he had enough for sure never to need it, and then, how he had turned it over to Laura and away it had gone. Gone fast, too, and he wondered was Laura really being careful of her spending. How he had stood around hemming and hawing and looking far-off when Mr. Johnson came again, waiting for him to slip him another, and then being mad when he didn't. Being mad when you didn't get charity—that was a pretty low comedown.

He leaned back against the tree, worn out, his leg thumping with pain, and let the team stray off down the fencerow. He lay down to rest a while but the sun shifted and bored through the branches as if it wanted to get a look at him. He tried to doze but he could hear that cowbell ringing in his head. Each of his hurts came back to him and he tried to recall the day it happened, hoping to remember something that might seem to deserve such punishment. The details of his troubles began crawling up over the edges of his mind and grew thick, like a gathering swarm of bees. It was not his family nor the people on the street—he was the one who had changed. Other men had troubles but they were separate and unconnected, each came and stung and went on. Something was wrong with a man when they came and did their hurt and then stayed, waiting for the next, until they'd eaten him hollow. He didn't have any troubles any more, he just had one big trouble. For a moment that gave him a sad thrill. He had been marked out. But why? He started to raise himself to see if the answer didn't lie somewhere near at hand, and halfway up was caught and held by the thought that nobody knew why, nobody could tell him. He lay back heavily and said aloud, "I probably have it all coming to me." It made him sad that he couldn't remember whatever he had done to deserve it.

They sat down to supper with Harold quiet and cautious. He had been punished for something and Dan felt like being sure he had deserved it. "What's wrong with him?" he asked.

Laura looked at Harold, waiting for him to speak up and declare how bad he had been and just what he had got for it. "He got a spanking," she said. Harold squirmed. Laura straightened him up with a look and said, "He got hisself a bell and went around ringing it all day. I asked him a hundred times to stop it but he wouldn't. I was jumping out of my skin all day long every five minutes thinking it was you and something bad had happened."

Dan threw his knife on his plate with a clatter. "Jesus Christ! Did you have it on your mind every minute that I was going to sound off on that damn thing!"

Laura bounced in her seat as if he had hit her; a slow hard pinch started in around the edges of her eyes. "Well, yes," she said, picking out all the bruises and breaks and bumps up and down him, "I did!"

VIII

Dan sat hunched up on the front porch, wandering wearily back and forth between the two minds he had about everything. He had sat there, just breathing, ever since they left, and now it was hard to believe that in the house behind his back anything had happened for years, or again, it seemed something had happened all right, the last thing that ever would, and now the house lay dead. Laura, she was down behind the barn, crying, he supposed, and one minute he would reckon he ought to stir himself and go out and try to comfort her, and the next minute figure he had just better keep out of her sight—not rousing himself to do either and not caring the next minute one way or the other, just wishing he could keep out of his own sight.

She was only going to take the boy over to her place until Laura had a little more time to spare him, the grandmother said, and Laura had taken no exception, even agreed with a tired nod that she hadn't given him much time of late and that Harold looked it every bit. It was not time she hadn't given him—though she hadn't given him that, either—and she knew it wasn't time or attention that his grandmother was thinking he needed. The old woman looked the boy over, tallying all the hollow spots that a few square meals would fill out. Her man was torn—strutting around throwing it up to Dan that he couldn't support his only child, pleased that *he* could, had figured for years that sooner or later he would have to, then suddenly fearing they might get to thinking he was better able to do it than he wanted them to think. Then he would pull a thin face to show how pinched he was going to be with his new responsibility.

Laura had followed them out to the buggy, wanting to say, We'll have you back soon, Harold, don't you worry. And afraid he would act as if that were the only thing that worried him. Suddenly she wanted to tell him that it wasn't any of her doing, that she wasn't that way, that there wasn't anything wrong with her—because he did look at her as though, since she was staying behind, the same thing must be wrong with her. Instead, settling him on the seat, not thinking, she said, "Drive careful, Papa."

She watched them move away and, turning, shoved the gate shut and watched it fall back in exhaustion. Walking up the path her words scraped dryly in her mind: Be careful, Papa. Be careful, careful, be careful. She came to the front steps and stood looking at Dan as she would at an old no-good hound dog lolling on the porch, then turned and walked around the house.

IX

That three acres of truck was not going to make a stand; they both saw that and so did Mr. Johnson. He hadn't got it in early enough and hadn't been able to work it like he should have, it had been too hot and dry or too cold and damp and it never got proper spraying and the bugs got at it and it wasn't a very good piece of land anyway and if anybody needed any more reason, well, it was his, and that ought to be enough.

They clung as long as they could, holding out against what they knew without saying was their only alternative. But a day came when the last piece of salt pork spread its weak stain through the last pot of beans, when the flour barrel was turned end up and dusted out on a newspaper, when you could just about see the blue flowers right through the pancakes on your plate, then, as if he had timed it to the last mouthful, Laura's papa pulled up outside the limp gate in his sway-backed wagon behind his draughty mules and sat up on the high spring seat looking down as though he might have revived things no end just by spitting on that ruined soil and wouldn't do it—which was a lie; he was so dried up himself he couldn't have brought up a nourishing spit. His face looked eroded and was covered with a maze of capillaries like exposed roots. On top of this a tangle of dry hair drifted like tumbleweed.

Behind him, piled among their battered belongings, Laura and Dan rode away without a backward glance.

He was hard up all right, Laura's papa, always had been, always would be, but his actual condition was never so low as you'd guess from the meal he gave them that first night. You would have thought he expected a bill collector for company. And he was upset that Laura's mama had put on such a good expensive-looking dress to welcome her daughter home and he found a way to remark two or three times about it being her only one. What it was was her very best guinea hen print and she sat puffed up in it all evening as if she had an egg but wouldn't lay it. As her husband offered the Lord his thanks for this and all His blessings—with a look at Dan—a scandalized look sneaked out of the corner of the old woman's eye and stole upward. She wanted Him and the others as well to know she hadn't forgot having had more in her day to thank Him for.

Dan guessed he'd never had more and they were all, it seemed, anxious to assure him that he never had. It looked as if her family had not only known him all his life but known him better than anyone else, better than he knew himself. They could recall accidents he had had and bring them clearly back to him, things he hadn't thought of for years, and now he supposed he had deliberately tried to forget them and had run for years from admitting this mark that was set on him, it seemed, the day he was born —and rolled out of his crib and got a knot on his head, the old man swore, and swore not to be mean, but you could tell from the look on his face, in genuine astonishment, it all added together so perfectly.

So perfectly it left not a minute's doubt in the mind of any of them that he was an absolute leper. Laura got tired of seeing him take it without any fight, but his time was taken up. Something would poke him awake in the morning, urge him to gulp down his coffee, so he could get started doing nothing and thinking nothing, and the effort of it had him worn out by evening. Everything everybody said or did was meant in some way for him, he felt, but it all had so little to do with him. Sometimes he felt like speaking up and getting in a dig himself at himself when they were all having such a good time running him down.

Laura believed he wasn't taking his position seriously enough. Instead of resenting her folks' charity as she had at first, she had come to feel they were being pretty nice to do all they had and that Dan might be decent enough to be grateful. He wasn't. They were getting their money's worth; they hadn't had anybody they could take as much out on in a long time. He had given them something more in common than they could ever have agreed upon amongst them. The bunch of them got along together now like fingers in a mitten.

At first Laura was always prophesying rain. If her papa was kept home then Dan wouldn't feel quite so bad that he wasn't out working. When it did rain she would pray for it to clear and get the old man back to the fields and out of the house where he couldn't torment Dan. The old man had the same problem rain or shine: Ought he to let them know how well the crops were coming for him—compared to *some* he could mention—or let them know what a lean winter they were in for around his table? He chose always to look worn to a frazzle; whichever way it turned out he had done his share and more.

Dan didn't care whether it rained or shone and he could see before long that Laura wasn't so worried one way or the other any more. Even with all she had to put up with from her mama, complaining about her cooking and the way she cleaned house and the grease she left around the sink and the way Harold dirtied his overalls so fast, with all that, Laura couldn't forget that she wasn't out forking hay or shaking out sods, couldn't feel any other way except that that was over now and she had come back home.

On the morning he was killed Dan woke earlier, struck with the thought he'd sooner spend the day with the old man than with the women. He went out to work a month before the date the doctor had set. He had expected it, but still it hurt when Laura didn't even try to stop him. She had seen him limp for so long she'd forgot there was a time when he didn't, couldn't believe a time might ever come when he wouldn't. He'd gone out too early before and the leg hadn't healed but it probably wouldn't have, anyway, and if it had something else as bad would have happened, if not worse.

How funny it was, Dan thought, that he didn't mind the old man now. It was clear that the old man despised him, and so it was no surprise to see that cowbell Laura had made him carry on Johnson's place hung under the mower that the old man meant for him to use. What did surprise Dan was that he didn't care. The old man stood by itching for a quarrel over it; Dan didn't have the energy.

He started in at one corner of the field and mowed three laps around. The steady clatter of the machine soothed him. With some surprise he had about decided that nothing out of the way was likely to happen when, near the end of his fourth time around, the mower bumped over a rock and he was thrown in front of the blade. The pointed runners held him spitted and the mules, taking fright, dragged him fifty feet before the spikes tore out and rolled over him.

He fought hard against coming to and half-conscious he knew he was badly hurt. He thought of what it was going to be like, dragging in bloody from head to toe, and he said to himself: Why can't I really have a good one once and for all and get it over with? He opened his eyes and looked at himself in disgust. Now, he thought, I'm going to catch hell sure enough. He started poking around in him for the strength to get up, but a wave of pain and sadness bent his will like the wind coming over the grass. If only he could just lie there and not have to go. But supposing they found him like this—that would be worse than if he dragged himself in. He tried to rise. But the grass came up cool and crisp, rustling like a fresh bedsheet, and tucked him in. What shall I dream about, he asked, and heard himself answer: You're already dreaming.

Then a voice like Mr. Johnson's said, "Are you going to lie there all day?" "No, sir, I'm going to get right up now and support my family."

He rolled over and groaned and opened his eyes. He could see the team a little ways off and was thankful for that bell hanging there. It cheered him so he got to his elbows and once he had he took a look at himself and laughed. If he could do that then he damned sure wasn't going to ring that bell. It would just be giving the old man too much to crow about. He looked again and wondered if he could have reached the bell anyhow, for there it went dancing all over the field.

Then Dan watched himself get up, get the bell and begin swinging it with all his might, pointing at the body on the ground as though he wanted everybody to come see what he had gone and done with himself now.

Report Cards

~~~~~~

Instead of calling the roll, Miss Carpenter peered over the rims of her glasses and said, "I suppose everyone is here." The groan that arose satisfied her that everyone was. There was a rustle of adjustment; the girls sighed and smoothed down their skirts; the boys coughed and squirmed and shuffled their feet. Only Thomas Erskine sat quietly, knowing he had nothing to fear.

"Grace Adams," Miss Carpenter called.

When Grace, on the way back to her seat, looked at her report card, she could not help smiling. Everyone was pleased for her.

Miss Carpenter bore hard on Jackie Barnes. Coolly, he put his into his pocket without a glance; that was showing her how much he cared.

Even Miss Carpenter had to give a smile for John Daniels. It was not how well he had done, just that he had passed was more than anyone expected. He grinned modestly from ear to ear.

Thomas only wished his mother could have heard the change that came into Miss Carpenter's voice when she called his name. He went up for his card, trying to look solemn and as though he did not understand the looks of hopeless envy on all the faces.

Then everyone looked busy or thoughtful to spare Miss Carpenter being watched at an unpleasant chore—it was time for the Hazeltines. Luther clomped up the aisle with his head hanging, took his card without looking up and clomped back to his seat. Then, without waiting to be called, as though she knew people preferred not to have to speak her name, Sal Hazeltine sidled up the aisle. She took her card and started back, then could not resist a look at it. She stopped. Her cheeks turned red. She began nibbling at the shreds of her chapped lips and blinking her eyes. Finally she remembered where she was, blushed a deeper shade, then hunched herself together and hurried back to her seat.

Thomas Erskine listened to her snuffling and thought with a shudder of the beating she would get when she got home. After today her parents need never give her another thought; she had lost her right to their affection. From now on even Luther, her own brother, would be ashamed to be seen with her. Her life here, he believed, was ruined; he could think of no way to make up for such a thing as Sal had done. That was what it meant to fail. At last he had seen it happen to someone. He might have known it would be Sal Hazeltine.

Yet, would such people as the Hazeltines care whether their child passed or failed? They would beat Sal for failing, but only because they never missed a chance to beat her, not because they really cared. Nor would they have cared very much if she had brought home straight A's. Imagining himself, for a moment, with such parents, seemed to Thomas the worst thing that might have happened to him in life.

154

He remembered coming home from school one afternoon and telling his mother, when she asked what happened in school that day, about Sal hemming and hawing and winding her skirt in her hand over a question so simple that probably even Luther knew the answer. They laughed together over the way Thomas imitated her. But one ought not to laugh, and straightening her face, Mother said, "Well, somebody loves her, I suppose." From the way she looked you could tell she thought it was hard to understand why.

While Miss Carpenter checked their books, examining the corners and giving the pages a quick but careful going-over, then checking off a name in her roll book, Thomas sat thinking about going to the country in just two days.

Virginia Tate was going to Hot Springs, Arkansas. Josephine Morris said her folks might go to New Orleans or maybe to Mexico. Everybody was going somewhere. Thomas was going to his grandmother's. They had talked about it before the bell rang, gathered on the school steps, the girls seated neatly on their handkerchiefs, the boys standing, everybody taking pains with clean linens and white shoes. A few feet away sat the Hazeltines. Everybody knew where *they* would spend the summer. Everybody could remember turning down the dusty road past the gravel pit, beyond the city-limit sign and driving past the Hazeltines' and seeing the scrawny razorback pig rooting wearily under the porch, the dusty, weathered old coonskins stretched on the walls of the house, and the Hazeltines stretched out on the front porch. Five or six or seven little Hazeltines would stop playing in the rusty old body of a model T Ford to stare at you through the thick white dust.

155

Richard Taylor was going to Carlsbad Caverns, and, oh, someone said, they were not so much. Just a lot of stalagmites and stalactites. And those who knew what those words meant took half a look and half a snicker at the Hazeltines, and so did those who no more knew than they.

Surely, thought Thomas, one day they would wake up, take a good look at themselves and then a look at the other children, and give up coming to school for shame. But they never missed a day. You might come ever so early, there they were—Sal in a molting straw hat and all that was left of a dress that once belonged to Jane Tucker, Luther in a floppy old leather chauffeur's cap and coveralls that had faded almost completely away.

Through the winter Luther smelled of stale Vick's salve, Antiphlogistine, Mentholatum. In the spring when all this lifted he was left smelling strongly of something that town people never ate—hominy. And Sal, because of the asafetida she wore in a little bag on a ribbon round her neck to keep away the croup, no one could get near Sal. At school they hung back and hung around and moved cautiously into a spot after the others had left it.

The Hazeltines. How could they not see all the things that were wrong with them?

Now they sat on the bottom step listening with their mouths hanging open while each told of the wonderful things he planned to see and do this summer. Finally, each trying to outdo the rest, everyone had told. A lull came, and the danger was that someone might mention report cards. Bobby Johnson nudged a couple of fellows and edged over toward the Hazeltines.

They looked up to see what was coming.

Smiling sweetly, Bobby Johnson said, "And where-all are you Hazeltines going to go this summer?"

156

The boys all simply yelped. The girls sniggered politely behind their hands. Some half got ready to run. Bobby Johnson looked like he wished he hadn't done it. For something down inside him gave a tug on Luther's Adam's apple. With his great callused hands, Luther could have wrung Bobby Johnson like a rag. But slowly a smile spread over Luther's face. He thought it was as good a joke as the rest. Then everybody really whooped. Sal grinned wider and wider; everybody was having such a good time; she was proud of Luther.

Oh, the Hazeltines! They were so dumb you simply could not insult them.

Thomas Erskine was miserable, though. No one hated the Hazeltines as much as he; the very sight of them embarrassed him. But he was miserable whenever they were tormented. He prayed that the Hazeltines might simply disappear. He hated the others for drawing attention to them, even if it was to make fun of them. He found himself hating their tormentors so much that he was almost sorry for Sal and Luther. To feel in himself a moment of sympathy for them, made him hate the Hazeltines all the more the next moment. On top of everything, he was terrified that someone might notice him not joining in the fun, might think back and realize that he had never joined in, then suspect him of liking the Hazeltines.

The bell rang. Thomas' relief was so great it left him feeling weak.

The Hazeltines' lunches always looked like something wrapped in newspaper to be disposed of. Across Sal's thin little bottom as she bent to pick hers up, you could read in faded letters, *Bewley's Best*.

Miss Carpenter opened the door and the children fell in line. Alphabetically the Hazeltines were entitled to march in behind Thomas Erskine. Everybody else had better fall in where he belonged. The Hazeltines, though, always marched at the rear, and Miss Carpenter never corrected them.

Luther sat behind Thomas, breathing noisily through his mouth. Behind him sat Sal, gulping softly with every breath. Thomas tried to get his mind on the country, on his bicycle, on his last birthday party. Finally he could hold off a certain thought no longer, a thought so painfully embarrassing that he could feel the blood rising up his neck and making his ears tingle. There would be many boys like Luther, openmouthed, overgrown country boys, and many weasel-faced little girls like Sal coming to Grandmother's farm during the summer to spend the day. Thieving along at their mothers' heels, they would be jerked forward to gawk at him and then be introduced by Grandmother as cousins of his.

They were very, very distant cousins, said Thomas' mother—so far removed nobody would think of counting it except old folks like Grandmother, who liked to keep track of such things.

Grandmother believed in owning all your kinships, but sometimes even she did not want to own to any more than she had to. "This is your fourth cousin Effie Hightower, Thomas," she would say. "And this is her little boy Ferris and that makes him your fifth cousin, I suppose." And she would smile at Effie's boy, glowering up at her like a gopher down a hole, as though he was lucky to be able to claim that much.

It was hard to smile all the way across a fourth cousinship.

Thomas lived in fear of the day when one of those

children might turn up at school and claim kin with him. It was bad enough already, with Aunt Jessie's boys there.

Aunt Jessie was Mother's sister, the one who had moved into town. She thought she dressed her boys in very townish clothes. Their great red hands hung out of their sleeves, their tight shoes squeaked with every step. Giles, Jess and Jules were their names.

Aunt Jessie was always thinking up things for Thomas and her boys to do together. It never seemed to bother her that Mother always found some way to get Thomas out of it. Aunt Jessie said she, too, had decided she didn't like her boys to play with any of their other cousins, and she was sure Harriet would understand what she meant.

"They are your nephews, you know, Jessie," said Mother. "The sons of your brothers and sisters."

"They are *our* nephews, Harriet," Aunt Jessie replied. "But I'm afraid there is nothing we can do about it."

To get his mind off all this, Thomas thought how proud his father would be of his report card. He would be bragging about it for weeks. He loved to have Thomas in the shop to show him off to friends, to have him near whenever he told a story. Then he would choose his words carefully, working his way around to some big word that Thomas had taught him lately. Sometimes, Thomas suspected, he used a word wrong deliberately, just so he could correct him. Then Father would turn to his friend with a look of wonder, as much as to say: Would you just look a-there! You and me, Joe, have been using that word wrong all our fool lives, and would be still if it wasn't for this boy of mine. He would say, "There. What did I tell you? I declare, Joe, this boy'll educate me yet."

When Father was eleven years old—and a little backward maybe, for even then he was only in low third, a big gangling boy and always in trouble, to hear him tell it—though Mother said he laid that on somewhat—he was taken out of school and put to work where there was cotton to hoe, sorghum to cut and wood to chop.

Thomas would have advantages, a headstart such as Father never had. Thomas knew very well how lucky he was; it was nice to visit the country, but what a wonderfully lucky thing that he had been born in town! His birthday came on June the eighteenth. One day more, they told him when he was little, and he would have been born black, for that was Emancipation Day. That was silly, of course, but the feeling he once got whenever they told him that was like the feeling that came over him when he thought what a lucky accident it was that he had been born in town.

Grandmother was just the other way. When she came up to town once every year or two, it was hard to get her to stay even overnight. "Don't coax me, Harriet," she would say peevishly, "I know very well I don't belong here and you don't need to worry that I'm going to stay very long." She would not wear the clothes Mother sent her for just that trip, but came in her country bonnet and her shoes with the left one slit for her bunion. And each such visit was her last. Never again, she would tell Thomas time after time through the summer he spent with her. She was going to sit right under the grape arbor where she belonged. Those that wanted to see her, if anyone did, could come out here, where she wouldn't be any embarrassment to them.

He would certainly come, Thomas said.

"Why?" she demanded. "To keep me from coming to your place?"

But she was not really as cross as she sounded. He knew, for Uncle Ben would wink at him when she got going like that, to remind him that that was just her way.

Uncle Ben made little boxes for Grandmother to cover with quilting and tassels and braid, making footstools one after another as she sat in her rocker in the arbor. He brought her milk bottles that she covered with plaster and into that set pretty stones and sea shells and bits of colored glass. He collected tin cans for the thing she liked best of all to do—cut the sides halfway down into thin shreds that curled up and made a ruff collar around the top. Wrapped with crepe paper and tied with ribbon, they made the prettiest flower pots. When Ben was too busy to find things for her she sent Thomas out to scout for snuff boxes that she decorated for holding collar buttons, though nobody used collar buttons any more. People who came to visit brought things for her that no one else, they said, could find any earthly use for, but that she would know how to make something pretty of.

Uncle Ben had an old car, but when his stay was up Thomas liked to be taken home in the buckboard. His things would be all packed in, Uncle Ben would climb up on the seat, Grandmother would kiss him and Grandfather shake his hand, then at the last minute Grandmother would make up her mind to send some little thing for Harriet. Thomas and the two men would wait while she went into the house, and all three were embarrassed. She would come back loaded down; she had so many and she had been unable to decide between three or four.

Riding in, Thomas held the reins while Uncle Ben enjoyed his tobacco. He chewed. And sometimes he spat long streams of juice, which was disgusting enough, but most of the time he swallowed it. Around ladies, to be polite, he swallowed. But around Harriet he never chewed at all, so as soon as they came in sight of Thomas' house he would clear his throat and spit out his wad and wipe his mouth. Then, reaching behind him, he would cover over Grandmother's gifts with a towsack or a tarpaulin. He pretended not to be doing anything and Thomas pretended not to notice, for they both knew that Mother always threw those things right out.

Wasn't that Katherine Spence? It was. She had left her car and was coming over to chat until the children were let out. Harriet found her left shoe under the clutch pedal and forced it on. She fluffed out her hair and gave Katherine just two minutes to work her way around to Our Walter. Had she told what our Walter came out with the other day? Did your Thomas ever do what our Walter did last week?

Harriet smiled. Didn't it go to prove something, the way women were always coming to her to talk about their children? It reminded her of an old colored woman who used to sit up on her front porch and explain the meaning of their dreams to darkies that came to her from miles around. For Katherine was only one of many. Harriet had noticed how the bridge women, and before them the forty-two club women, could talk among themselves about other things, but turning to her they invariably got off on the subject of children. She could not help feeling they wanted to check and see how theirs were coming along compared to Thomas Erskine at a certain age.

Katherine Spence came and stood with her foot on the running board, chatting away and trying to be carefree, but really nervous and hot and tired. The poor thing was Harriet's own age and looked five years older.

162

"Harriet," she said, interrupting herself in the middle of something to which she herself was not paying any attention, "I don't know how you manage to always look so cool and collected. All I can say is, you're lucky you don't have three of them." Which was her way of saying she felt lucky that she did. Katherine was known to think that having had three children showed she had been well able to afford them.

Katherine Spence was from a good old family, long settled in town. And here she was now, envying Harriet for being so cool and collected. Who could have predicted it, to see them when they were in grammar school together, where Katherine was one of the cruel little town girls, all cool and prim and sweet-smelling in their stiff Kate Greenaways, that grimy little Harriet Purdy wanted so much to be like? Harriet began to feel rather warm toward Katherine. To ask after her children gave her a charitable glow. Were they looking forward to vacations? Mercy yes, *they* were—but as for herself—

How awful, how guilty it must make you feel, thought Harriet, to know that you would feel relieved to be rid of your children for the summer. She said, "Well, if Thomas was like other children so you could get his nose out of a book once in a while and send him out to run and play, then I wouldn't let him go to the country for the summer. But he always comes back looking so good, it seems selfish of me not to want him to go." She smiled at the sight of him in her mind, so fresh and rosy and filled-out.

"Well," Katherine sighed, "all I can say is, you're lucky to have a place to send him and know he's safe without worrying every minute."

Without worrying! As if she would get a wink of sleep all summer! All she had been able to think about lying awake at night for the last two weeks was all the terrible accidents she'd seen happen to her brothers when they were boys. She would never have said such a thing, of course, and even to think it seemed wrong, but that did not keep her from feeling that Katherine, nor any other woman, did not know what it was to worry over a child!

Harriet was pleased when Katherine Spence left. She soon grew tired of listening to women talk about their children. She found it hard to follow, never having in mind a very clear picture of their children. That was because to think of children automatically got her mind on Thomas.

At seven months he had talked. Immediately he knew eleven words and from the very first there was never a baby flavor to his speech. Often as Harriet called that to mind, it never failed to surprise and please her. The reason for it was, she had never spoken baby talk to him and never allowed anyone else to, so much as a word. At eight months and three days he said, "Oh, look at the dog."

What a shame it was, thought Harriet for the hundredth time, that the classes were attuned not to the quickest, but to the very slowest pupils.

At last the doors were opened and the children tumbled out. How loud and rough they were! Harriet hardly saw them, but looked over them, around and through them impatiently. Then, there he was! Each time she saw him was a surprise. He is mine, she told herself; I am responsible for him. But she felt she would never get quite used to the idea.

He walked down the steps with his shoulders square, very dignified and grownup. Before long he would be changing to knickers, then long pants before you knew it. He did look sweet in short pants, his knees were never scuffed, his stockings never sagged.

164

The compliments she had had on him would fill a mail-order catalogue. His fine nose, his high clear forehead and long lashes were like no one else's in her family, thank goodness, and certainly not like anyone's in his father's. He was fair, almost pale. Not sickly-looking, but not a big freckle-faced bumpkin. He never had a cowlick. Everybody wondered how she kept his hair always so neat. In fact, in every way he was something to wonder over. In fact, thought Harriet, he was the absolute despair of every other mother in town.

Thomas said, "Miss Carpenter wants to see us both in her office."

Miss Carpenter's office was a dark room with a wall map and an old globe. It was a room which once held terrors for Harriet and it gave her a funny feeling now. She was amazed how little it had changed since the day she came there to tell old Miss Briggs that she was being taken out of school. Harriet had been through four grades, which was four more than anybody else in the whole connection, her father said, and as many as he could afford. She had expected Miss Briggs to see how cruel that was and to say that she would speak to her father. She had broken down and sobbed. And then Miss Briggs had said, in what she meant to be a soothing tone, "Well, Harriet dear, I guess it *is* enough, really, for living on a farm." She wished it was Miss Briggs sitting there now so she could see the change in things.

"Mrs. Erskine," said Miss Carpenter, "I, and Thomas' other teachers, have been watching him closely this year, and we feel that he is decidedly in advance of his class."

Harriet sat quietly and tried to look solemn. But she had to grin. The next minute she felt a pang of disappointment that no one else was there to hear.

Miss Carpenter brought out her roll book. "Erskine, Thomas," she read. "Class response—at random: 99, 98, 97, 99, 96, 98."

Miss Carpenter never gave 100's, Harriet reflected. No one was perfect, she maintained.

"Music 96, Geography 98, English 98—but you know all this, of course," said Miss Carpenter, and Harriet nodded, though she would not have minded hearing more of them read out. Miss Carpenter closed the book. "So we feel, Mrs. Erskine, that with your permission—for we don't want you to feel we're rushing him—we might give Thomas a try at high fifth next year."

From now on, Harriet sat thinking, he would do three semesters in every two. Think how young he would be to enter college!

"Well, how do you feel about this, Thomas?" she said.

He was thinking back through the year, trying to find what he had done to deserve this. He had studied every night and raised his hand for every question. But he had done all that before, too, and not been double-promoted. What more could he do to be sure of getting double-promoted again next year?

"Perhaps," said Miss Carpenter kindly, "perhaps Thomas feels sad at the thought of leaving all his little friends behind."

Tommy smiled faintly. Harriet smiled broadly, delighted with the thought of his leaving them behind.

"Well," said Harriet, "Thomas will soon make new friends in high fifth."

"Then it's all settled," said Miss Carpenter rising.

She asked them to wait one moment. She lifted the wall map that hung in front of a bookcase. She fitted her glasses and peered into the dark shelves until she found

166

the book she wanted and brought it out, blowing dust off it.

"Here," she said to Thomas, "something to keep you busy for a while." For Miss Carpenter barely tolerated summer, a season of laziness good only for making children forget all that she had taught them the year before.

Walking down the quiet halls Thomas thought how neither his father nor his mother had ever got as far in school as he was now. He could understand Harriet's pride in him. But he wished she wouldn't show it so plainly. It was not modest and it was not refined. He hoped she was not going to make too much over this in front of other people. Whenever she did that it made him embarrassed for her and angry, afraid that people thought he enjoyed being shown off. For her to make so much over it seemed to reveal that she herself had never had much schooling.

One minute Harriet was glad that no one else knew about this, so she could have all the pleasure of telling it, and the next minute it seemed impossible that the news was not already all over town.

As they reached the steps she threw back her head and laughed. "Just wait till I tell Jessie!" she cried. "Can't you just see the look on her face!"

To Thomas this sounded exactly like the sort of thing Aunt Jessie herself might have said, and a tremor of shame ran through him.

Harriet thought of the letter she would write her family. She could see her mother and father and Ben and all the rest of them sitting, reading it aloud, growing madder by the minute, until one of them said, "Well, you know Harriet. She would say anything in the world just to be different from the rest of us."

"I guess you're mighty proud of yourself, aren't you?"

she said, feeling actually that he did not seem nearly as proud as he ought. "Why, when I was a little girl," she said, and her voice began trailing, growing faraway and sad, as it did whenever she spoke of her childhood.

They passed the lonely seesaws and the swings hanging deadened and stiff. Down at the far corner of the playground, leaning against a slide, the Hazeltines sat waiting for somebody to come get them, chewing on their peanut butter sandwiches, watching the cars go by.

"Why, when I was a little girl," she said, "if I'd got double-promoted, why, I'd have been so proud of myself nobody could have come near me."

The Fauve

~~~~~~

M r. Emmons the butcher no longer smiled or shook his head in sympathy, and certainly he never brought down his price on anything when Rachel Ruggles said, "Oh, dear . . ."

It embarrassed Rachel to have to sigh over the prices of things. She dreamed of a time when she would be able simply to pay what was asked for things. But each time she went shopping she found prices a little higher.

Mr. Emmons shifted from foot to foot while Rachel stood looking at the meats in the counter. It took her a long while, not to choose, but to resign herself to another week of lung stew.

While Mr. Emmons wrapped her order Rachel allowed herself to gaze at the lamb chops. James craved lamb chops. So, although lamb chops had been beyond their means for years, Rachel felt sad each time the price of them went up. And the more expensive they became the more she admired James for his expensive tastes.

From Emmons' Market Rachel went down the street to the Universal Union store.

For years Rachel had wished for a supermarket in Redmond. When the baker first quit giving baker's dozens,

169

when the butcher began charging for marrow bones, she sighed, "If only there were a supermarket in town." Finally a Universal Union was built. Rachel had been astonished to find that the prices there were still more than she could afford.

But hope was always strong in Rachel. Before each shopping trip she convinced herself that this time she would find prices within her budget. Then she would come upon soup which had been nine cents a can last week and now was eleven. Other women begged her pardon, reached around her and took two, three, four cans of soup while she hesitated. Sometimes she felt she was the only woman in the world who had to watch her pennies.

Today, however, at the Universal Union Rachel found day-old bread at half-price, a one-cent sale on soap and a special on sugar—so many bargains that she decided to buy some little treat for James. He loved artichokes. She picked out two. As the clerk was putting them into a bag she said:

"Oh, wait. That one is bruised."

The clerk said, "I'll get you another instead."

"I suppose part of it is all right," she hinted. "If I just took off the top leaves."

The clerk said nothing. He stood waiting. She was about to suggest he let her have it for half-price. Suddenly she imagined James watching her. She said hurriedly, "Never mind. Just give me the good one."

The clerk shrugged his shoulders. Rachel took the bag, wondering what she was going to do with one artichoke. The clerk picked up the bad one, looked at it, then, as Rachel was turning away, tossed it into the wastebasket.

Rachel almost gasped. A perfectly good artichoke! Her next thought was of James. What if he knew she had haggled over something for him which a clerk considered fit for the trash!

Standing there, Rachel could not help thinking that if she asked him, the clerk would probably give her that artichoke. James need never know. It was selfish of her to rob him of such pleasure merely to spare herself a little embarrassment.

Rachel shook her head to get such thoughts out of her mind, and wheeled away her carriage to put herself out of range of temptation. She shuddered to think of serving James that artichoke, and him finding out. And she was convinced that with his fine taste he would know. She was even afraid he would be able to tell that she had had these thoughts.

But Rachel could not worry or remain unhappy for long. She walked down the street enjoying the air and the early sunlight, and even seeing onions cheaper than she had just paid could not put her out of humor.

Many of the shops were just opening. The blinds went up in the bakery and the door was opened to let the smell of fresh bread settle heavily on the street. Mrs. Burton, her hair in curlers, leaned out of the window of her apartment over the variety store and shook the breakfast crumbs out of a red-checked tablecloth. On the sidewalk in front of the hardware store the clerk was setting out spades and turning forks and flats of pale tomato plants. The sun moved from behind the spire of the church and lighted the new glass onyx front of the drug store, and the china, the milk glass and the brassware in the window of the antique shop.

Suddenly from around a corner rolled a truck loaded with men in overalls. It pulled up in front of the old Redmond Inn. The men piled out and began unloading tool

171

kits, while a fat man from the cab of the truck stood surveying the building with his hands on his hips. The men
rummaged in their kits and came up with hammers, chisels
and wrecking bars.

A young man shinnied up a porch pole to the weather-
beaten sign of the Inn, and motioning those below aside,
raised his hammer. But the sound of a blow was heard
while his hammer was still poised. The men turned to
look up the street. The crew hired to demolish the old
Putnam Tavern had beaten them to the job this morning.

Soon, thought Rachel, all the old landmarks would be
known only in pictures. In the early days there had been
so many things in Redmond to paint. That was why it had
been chosen as a colony. One of the most popular subjects
was the Inn. James was perhaps the only painter in town
who had never done a picture of it. Among the artists the
saying was, you can always sell a picture of the Inn. Rachel
herself had painted it many times. It was ironical that all
those pictures of the Inn and the Tavern and the old mill
had brought so much money to Redmond that now it had
no room for old unprofitable buildings and was tearing
them down two or three at a time to make way for movie
houses and tea rooms and ski-supply stores. It was becoming hard for Rachel to remember Redmond as it looked
when she first came. And according to James a great deal
of the charm was gone already when she got there.

"Good morning, Rachel."

"Oh, good morning, John."

"Fine morning."

"It certainly is. How are Mary and the children?"

"Fine, thanks. Just fine."

Rachel had not gone five steps when she recalled that
she was not supposed to be friendly with John Daniels.

What a nerve he had, saying Mary was fine! What could one trust? Rachel asked herself. John Daniels was known as a great family man—and all those years he had been beating his wife every Saturday night! Oh, it seemed that every day one discovered fresh wickedness in the world. And what she knew was only a fraction, even, of what went on in Redmond, for James protected her from the knowledge of so much more. It was for her peace of mind that he never told her about John Daniels until last week, though he had known it for years. James was so considerate. I, too, Rachel told herself, might have got a man who beat me. The more she lived and the more she saw of the world, the more sure she was that hers was the best man alive.

"Rachel, you're looking mighty cheerful this morning." It was Martha Phillips.

"Martha!" cried Rachel. "Just the person I was hoping to see. I've been dying to tell you what happened with James and me the other day."

"Don't tell me you've left him," said Martha.

"Martha!" said Rachel. "Now what I wanted to tell you was about a little misunderstanding we had the day before yesterday. It was in the morning. Then . . ."

"You're welcome to come to my place, Rachel. I've got an extra . . ."

"Wait, let me finish. It was nothing important, you understand."

"Well," said Martha, "just remember, if he ever . . ."

"Let me finish, Martha. Listen. I don't even remember what we disagreed over. The important thing is what happened in the afternoon. James said he knew he had been short-tempered with me lately, and asked me to forgive him. 'Don't say I haven't,' he said, 'because I know I have.'

173

And he said that now at last he could tell me the reason."

Rachel paused to get her breath, then emphasizing each word, "He said that for the last six months he had been tormented with the fear that he loved another woman!"

"What!" cried Martha. "Who?"

"Wait, wait. Then he said, 'Well, I know better now. I thought I was in love with Jane Borden,' he said, 'but now I realize it was only her money I was in love with.'"

"Ah-hah," said Martha. "And now that all of a sudden she hasn't got any any more he knows it wasn't love."

"Oh, Martha, imagine him living in that torment all that time! Not knowing how he felt, doubting himself at every turn, not wanting to hurt me." Rachel's eyes moistened, she was silent for a moment, then she sighed, "And when I think how it is with some couples."

"You have," asked Martha, "some particular couple in mind?"

"Martha, would you ever think to look at him that every Saturday night for the last ten years John Daniels has beaten Mary!"

"What! John Daniels! Oh, Lord! Who ever told you that one?" cried Martha. "Why, if anything, Mary beats him!"

Rachel was confused. She changed the subject. She said, "Martha, I've got a little laugh on James. I didn't tell him, you understand, but I hadn't noticed he was being short-tempered with me lately. Had you, Martha?"

"Oh, Rachel, Rachel," Martha laughed, and went off down the street shaking her head.

Rachel liked to spread her shopping over all the stores in town. It made her feel she was buying more. She spent ten cents here, twenty-five there, and thought that in so doing she kept a good name with each merchant. It was eleven o'clock by the time she finished. She started home.

Rounding the curve in Main Street she was delighted to see James strolling into town. His migraine must have passed. She set down her packages and waved to him. He came on at the same pace. He sparkled in the sunshine, with his pink cheeks and his orange curls. "James Finley Ruggles," said Rachel to herself.

He was a big man with a slow stride. He wore red mustaches trained into a cheerful twirl. His tweed jacket was ancient; fuzzy and gray, it seemed to have sprouted a mold. The sleeves came down no further because they had grown frayed and been turned back more than once. His trousers had once been some other color, now they were more pale pink than anything else. Too short, they revealed Argyle socks of red and yellow.

Gathering up her packages, Rachel hastened to meet him.

"James," she called, "I got an artichoke," and fumbling in the bag as she walked, she found it and brought it out and bore it before her. "See?"

"I never knew you liked them," said James.

She came to a stop. "It's for you."

"*All* of it?"

Rachel looked at it. It seemed to shrink.

"With lung stew?" said James, clearing his throat.

She had not thought of that. She looked again at the artichoke. Then she found James smiling tolerantly at her, as though having asked himself how she could be expected to know any better.

She did not say how glad she was to see him up. James never liked to have it observed that he had got over an illness. Rachel was pleased with herself for having discovered this little quirk of his. She had a little hoard of such insights. She admired him for being complicated.

James said there was a meeting of the Artists' Association, and set off. Rachel hitched up her packages and followed, taking two steps to his one.

Rachel thought that when they walked together they made quite a handsome pair. She thought she set James off well. She was dark as he was fair. Her eyes, set in slanted lids, were as intensely black as his were blue. Her hair, glossy black and straight, parted in the middle and gathered into a heavy bun, was the perfect complement to his mass of orange ringlets. It was with an eye to James's clothes that she had made her lowcut flowing peasant blouse with its rich embroidery, and her long skirt of thick blue flannel.

As she walked Rachel was trying to think of someone to talk to James about. He had standards so high that few people could come up to them. Rachel was aware that she had no standards at all; but for James she would have let herself like just anybody. So she mentioned names to him, hoping always to have luckily hit upon a person really worthy. She said cheerfully, "I saw Martha Phillips this morning, James."

He sighed. "Drunk as usual, I suppose."

"Drunk?" cried Rachel. "Why, I never knew Martha drank. Martha Phillips, James?"

"Phillips, yes. That's what she calls herself now."

"Now? What do you mean 'now'? Why, I've known Martha Phillips for . . ."

"Yes—many people have known Martha. Many people —and many places."

"Martha *Phillips*, James? Why . . ."

"Well," he said, "you've got to give the old girl credit.

She's managed to keep her many lives pretty well apart all these years. Not many people know about that old Mexico City business."

"Many lives?" gasped Rachel. "Old Mexico City business? Why, James, you simply take my breath away."

"So what did she have to say?" asked James. "If it's fit to repeat."

"You've got me so confused I can't remember. But she laughed when I told her about John Daniels."

"One is bound to laugh, Rachel, at anything about John Daniels. Exactly what do you mean?"

"Why, Martha said if anything Mary beats him."

"You didn't know that?" asked James.

"But, James," she cried. Her head was reeling. "You told me . . ."

"Why, on Saturday nights you can hear them all over town. She ties him to a bedpost and beats him with a coathanger and shouts filthy names at him while he cries, 'Harder! Harder!' "

Rachel stood shaking her head and gasping.

"If she didn't satisfy him that way," said James, "God knows what he'd be out doing."

"Really, James?" said Rachel. "*Really?*"

James sighed. "Rachel," he said, "do you have to believe every word I say?"

"You mean it isn't true?"

"Of course it's true," he said.

They walked on, Rachel still trying to think of someone worth mentioning to him, but afraid to mention anyone now.

James was thinking about himself. He pictured himself walking into the Artists' Association meeting. During the three months between these meetings he saw little of the

177

other artists in town. Since the last one many things had happened. David Peterson had won five thousand dollars at the Carnegie International. The Cleveland Museum had paid two thousand dollars for one of Carl Robbins' watercolors. Most everyone had had exhibitions.

The faces of the people he was about to see came into his mind, and as they did he seated them one by one around a banquet table. It was a surprise party. On the walls of the room his pictures were hung in thick gold frames. A toast was proposed. To James Finley Ruggles! Everyone drank. Then the table fell quiet. A page boy entered and approached James, bearing a tray on which lay a book. The title was *James Finley Ruggles: A Tribute.* He looked around the table, remembering the struggle he had had, the years of working and waiting. Yet he felt no rancor toward these men, each of whom had been so slow in recognizing his superiority. A lump came into his throat. "Open it!" a shout went up. He read the table of contents: "My friend Jim Ruggles" by Pablo Picasso; "To JFR from H. Matisse: Greetings"; "James Finley Ruggles, the First Thirty Years" by the Staff of the Museum of Modern Art; "Ruggles and Cézanne" by Sheldon Cheney. . . .

In the book was a biographical sketch.

James Finley Ruggles, the fourth to bear that name, was born in Wellfleet, Massachusetts, on the night of September 22, 1904. The doctor gave no hope for him. The nurse, not so easily discouraged, blew into the infant's lungs time after time. That nurse blew the breath of life into American painting.

The Finleys were descended from a charter member of the Harvard Corporation. They were a family of doctors and brokers, shippers and tea importers. General Isaiah Ruggles was with Washington at Valley Forge.

To the public school teachers of Wellfleet the future artist seemed backward. He drew pictures on the pages of his arithmetic text. Plate 10 is a copy of a Raphael drawing that Ruggles made at the age of eight.

His was the classic story of the misunderstood artist. His father insisted that he enter the family insurance firm, badly in need of new blood. James was sent to Bowdoin, where all the Ruggles had been educated.

His legacy upon the death of his father in 1925, though not as large as he had expected, was enough to take him to Paris, where he studied for two years.

Upon returning to this country he lived for a while in New York, then went to join the artists' colony at Redmond. There he entered upon his Modified Fauve period, producing his first major works.

In Redmond, fame and money came to the third-rate all about him while Ruggles struggled against poverty and neglect. The epoch-making *Still Life with Pineapple* was rejected by every major exhibition jury in the country. But though accustomed to ceremony and tradition, to ease and gracious living, Ruggles bore his poverty lightly. A gay and colorful figure, he brought to Redmond the charm and gallantry and the cultivation of his aristocratic background. His wit was legendary and—

"James," said Rachel, "where are you going? Here we are."

His wife Rachel, née Ravich, was the eighth child of Solomon and Sarah Ravich, of Delancey Street and Brownsville, Brooklyn.

The doors of the meeting hall were not yet open, so everyone was gathered in the gallery lounge to chat. A heavy layer of smoke hanging just above their heads rocked lazily each time the door was opened. People drifted from one group to another as though they, too, were stirred by the wind from the door. The talk rose and fell.

How fat they were all becoming, thought James, how bourgeois. The men in double-breasted suits and suède shoes, the women with Florida suntans gave it the look of a convention of fashion buyers.

The Ruggles stood while James singled out someone to approach. An aisle fell open revealing David Peterson at the end of the room. But before they could reach him they were stopped by Mary McCoy.

"Mary, you've done something to your hair," said James. She certainly had, and Rachel was alarmed at his drawing attention to it. "You always did have the prettiest head of hair in town, and now it's even nicer."

The truth was, her hair was probably the least attractive of poor Mary's features. It was James's way with women always to flatter them where they most needed it. No harm was done if, on the side, it amused him to do it.

"It's a regular rat's nest," said Mary.

"Well, of course," said James, "you may be right. I'm no expert," and having spied an opening to Douglas Fraleigh he left her to regret not leaving well enough alone. When he offered to flatter someone he did not like her to try to draw more out of him. Besides, he really enjoyed flattering only people who did not need it, who were indifferent to flattery.

Douglas Fraleigh finished the story he was telling and left his listeners to laugh while he turned. "Oh, hello, Ruggles," he said.

"That's a nice suit," said James.

Fraleigh thanked him, making little effort to suppress a smile over James's garb. But it was lost on James. He was fascinated by Fraleigh's suit. He reached out his hand and Fraleigh suffered him to finger the cloth of the lapel. It was soft, dark flannel, glowing brown with a tasteful light stripe. The sight and feel of fine cloth brought to James's eyes a glossy, vacant look. As he fingered it he could feel the cloth upon his own skin. He was born for soft, luxurious fabrics.

There came to his mind the image of himself in the rags in which he stood. James had suffered at being Bohemian when everyone in Redmond was. Now that he was the only one he suffered intensely.

Douglas Fraleigh gave a twitch, a cough. James recovered himself to see one of Fraleigh's knees twitching with impatience inside his trousers. There was a tolerant, bemused smile on Fraleigh's lips.

James drew himself up, proud of his rags. He had known the best. He would rather know the worst than this tawdry in-between. Thank God he didn't look like Fraleigh and the rest of these parvenus! He promised himself to dress even more outrageously from now on. He was the only one in the room you would have known for an artist. And what suits he would have someday! So tasteful, of such elegant simplicity.

"Nice," he said with a gesture at Fraleigh's suit. "Just be careful not to let it get wet."

James drifted about. Time was running out and here he had alienated somebody, when he had meant to do just the opposite. He could not settle on the one person most worth his efforts.

It was growing hot in the room and the restraint wearing off. The little groups were dissolving, melting together, and the conversation becoming general. It took a while for these people to warm up to each other. No doubt they had all known each other too well in their days of communal poverty and Bohemianism. More than one was resentful that to those close to him he was not as legendary as he had become to the world at large.

They had had too many things in common ever to trust one another. Too many women, for example, such as Bertha Wallace. Bertha had posed for them all, and been the mistress of many of them. She was still far from unattractive. But Bertha was resentful of the men who had painted all those famous pictures of her, and who wanted to paint her no longer. Now that the Redmond Inn was being torn down she needed a place to live. She felt it was up to the painters she had helped make famous to find one for her. She must have been drinking heavily all morning and now as she circulated among them she had worked herself up into the conviction, never far from her at any time, that they owed her not only a roof but a living as well. "Where would you be," she demanded of Carl Robbins, hanging on to his lapel and thrusting her face up into his, "I'd just like to know where you'd be if it wasn't for *Portrait of Bertha, Bertha in a Yellow Gown, Bertha Reclining?*"

"You're right, Bertha, you're right," Carl Robbins tried to quiet her. He looked about him for help, and all the men who owed Bertha just as much, or as little, as he did, turned away and became suddenly absorbed in their conversations.

James found himself being vigorously shaken by the hand of Sam Morris.

Morris was the town doctor. But he refused to let anyone call him Doctor. "The name is plain Sam," he insisted. When Morris came to Redmond a few years back he painted only on Sundays. Now, the joke went, he was a Sunday doctor. At first a timid man, impressed into silence by his slavish respect for the artists, he had grown more and more talkative until now he started babbling the minute he stepped up and never let the other person say a word. He had been brought to this by one of the great disillusionments of his life. He had read all the great critics, subscribed to all the art magazines and read each from cover to cover, knew more about the history of Impressionism than any man alive—only to find that the artists never mentioned these things, but insisted on telling him of their migraines, the traces of albumen in their urine, their varicose veins. Now he had come to be suspicious that when they praised his painting they were only working their way around to wheedling some medical advice.

No one praised his art more extravagantly than James Ruggles, nor did Ruggles ever seem to have an ache or a pain. His other reason for liking Ruggles was that he *looked* like an artist.

"You're busy I know," he said, "but you must take just an hour some day to let me show you what I've been doing lately. I flatter myself that my late work is not without some sign of your influence. It's in the way you handle three-dimensionality."

As he talked he kept admiring James's clothes with one eye. One could tell he was thinking that but for his wife he, too, would let himself go like that, be really unconventional, really look like an artist. James could not help feeling somewhat flattered, but not enough to overcome his annoyance. James hated anyone who painted, but he hated more someone who spent only part-time at it. Moreover, he considered it a pitiful spectacle, a man who was a member of a solid respectable profession taking up painting.

When Morris finally left him the first person James saw was Max Aronson. Aronson stood to one side, neglected, a sad-faced, nervous little man with his hands to his mouth, gnawing a fingernail. He beamed when he saw James approaching.

"That was quite a spread you got in *Life*, Max," said James.

"Did you like it? The color reproductions were good, didn't you think?"

James said he thought they were.

"You really liked it, then?"

This little man, one of the most famous painters in the country, did not distinguish among the people who praised him. He lived on praise. Now, praise was the thing that came easiest to James Ruggles' lips. He liked to be amiable that way. But he thought everybody understood that it was to be taken for amiability and nothing more. To find somebody taking his flattery seriously shocked him. He was not giving out art criticism when he praised you. He was being a likable fellow.

"You really liked it, huh, James?" Max implored. "Tell me the truth now. I'd like to know what you really think."

James could not bear the sight of such naked hunger for praise. "I liked it," he said, tugging at his mustache. "You understand, of course, that I'd say so whether I thought it or not."

Max laughed, trying to make a joke of it.

The doors of the meeting hall were thrown open.

Scanning the room, James found the seat next to David Peterson empty. He grabbed Rachel's arm, and apologizing in advance as he pushed people aside, elbowed his way down the aisle. A man was just stepping into the row where Peterson sat. James got behind Rachel and shoved her into the man. Rachel blushed and began stammering apologies. The man glared, then gave a strained smile and stepped aside to let her enter. She started to, but James laid a hand on her arm. With a smile at the gentleman and a nod of thanks, he went in first and walked serenely down to the seat beside Peterson. Rachel followed, upsetting the hats of the ladies in the next row down as she smiled apologies back to the gentleman on the aisle.

"Dave!" cried James. "I thought it was you. Well, this is luck. Hello! Haven't seen you since the big news. Congratulations." He nudged Rachel.

"Yes! Congratulations!" she said.

"Yes, indeed," said James. "The Carnegie International! How does it feel to be world-famous?"

Peterson wound his watch, smiled uncomfortably and crossed and recrossed his legs, trying, as James knew, to keep his eyes off James for fear of bringing attention to his clothes.

"It must have come like a bolt from the blue," James went on, growing louder.

Peterson smiled agreeably. But he did not think it had come quite that unexpectedly, to him or to the world.

"Well, well, well," said James. "Old David Peterson! And I knew him when. Who would ever have thought it?"

People were beginning to turn to look. Peterson grew still more uncomfortable.

"I suppose the money's spent by now," said James. He gave a hearty laugh that made Peterson squirm. "That's not a question," he added hurriedly. "I'm not prying." He slapped Peterson's knee. "But you understand that, of course, Dave." He was sickening himself with his loud, back-slapping familiarity. "Well, all things come to him who waits."

Peterson obviously felt that he had hardly waited all *that*

185

long. He was not so old. "How has your work been coming,
James?" he asked.

"Oh! Don't ask after *my* work!"

"Don't be modest," said Peterson. "I'm sure you've been
doing fine work, as always."

This was sincere. David Peterson had always admired
James Ruggles' painting, and had put in a good word for it
in places where he knew it could never be popular, even in
places where he was not likely to make himself more popular by praising it. But James would never know that. James
did not mind giving praise, but he hated to receive it. It
never occurred to him that praise could be sincere.

He smiled, but such a savage smile that Peterson drew
back, wounded. He felt he deserved some credit for being
one of the very few men in Redmond who appreciated
James's work.

"It must be hard now," said James, "for you to remember
the days when we . . ."

David Peterson remembered all too well the days when
he resembled James Ruggles. He did not like to be reminded and he curled his lips to say something cutting.
Then he felt ashamed. He had risen and he had a lot to be
thankful for. His face relaxed. James followed all these
feelings of Peterson's and he foresaw his next. The man
was about to take pity on him, to offer to pull strings.
James began to twitch. He stuttered, trying to find something to say quickly. "Well, how's—ah!—hmm—well, where
are you— Oh! there's the chairman!" he almost shouted,
and breathed a sigh of relief.

The chairman pounded the table with his gavel and
when the crowd became quiet he announced that a letter
had been received from the trustees of the Walter Fielding estate offering to the Redmond Gallery a fund of

three thousand dollars annually to be awarded to the winners of the Redmond Exhibition.

There had never been any selection of winners in the annual exhibition. It had been simply a time to show one's work, with no jury, no prizes, no awards. The rule of the Gallery from the day of its founding had been to show everything. Anyone who lived in Redmond and who had ever painted a picture could hang it in the annual exhibition.

Now, if the Redmond Gallery wanted to accept the fund from the Fielding estate a jury would have to be chosen. It should have been done long ago, said the chairman. For, said he, the Redmond Gallery had come to have a responsibility to the country, indeed, to the world, and could not afford to hang pictures that brought laughter and ridicule to it. He threw the matter open to the floor. Two or three men got up to voice their approval. Someone put it in the form of a motion. It was quickly seconded.

"Further discussion?" asked the chairman.

"Mr. Chairman." This voice was deeper, more authoritative than the others. Everyone turned. James was on his feet, his arms folded across his chest. The chairman's eyes grew wide with apprehension. An embarrassed silence fell on the audience and people looked avertedly at one another.

"Mr. Chairman," said James, then turned his gaze upon the crowd. "Friends and fellow artists. At the risk of repeating what many of you have heard me say too often already—" He paused to allow them to chuckle. The silence was intense. "Well, anyway, let me say that it is indeed time that the Redmond Gallery came of age."

A man from the audience tiptoed up to the chairman

and drew him close, and as he whispered in his ear they both watched James from the corners of their eyes.

"The walls of this gallery are sacred space," James said. "I have observed with alarm the increasing amount of that space given over in past exhibitions to the work of—well, let us speak frankly—to the 'work' of amateurs and dabblers."

While catching his breath James observed Sam Morris nodding in agreement.

"It begins to seem," said James, "that everyone thinks he is a painter."

The silence was broken by a snigger unmistakably ironical.

"The walls of the Redmond Gallery," James was becoming passionate now, "are being taken over by retired school teachers, superannuated bank clerks and unemployed schizophrenics."

He gave a laugh, which fell upon the silence with a dying ring, like a coin dropped on a counter.

"Now I have nothing against these classes of people," he said. "Some of my best friends, you know. But I hardly think their daubs deserve to hang alongside the work of serious painters, men who have given their lives to painting. There must always be room in the Redmond Gallery for painters of different persuasions, but the painters of Redmond have suffered enough laughter and ridicule and indignity by hanging alongside the dabblings of amateurs and neurotics! And so, ladies and gentlemen, I wholeheartedly endorse the recommendation to elect a jury, and I am sure you will all follow me in supporting this much-needed reform."

Conscious of the silence, which he took for a hushed admiration, he closed on a rising note, then lowered his

gaze to the audience to receive their smiles of approval.
Instead, he saw upon their faces looks of uneasiness, and
embarrassment, blank stares. His smile began to give way
to confusion. The silence deepened. He brought his eyes
to focus upon the faces nearer him. As he stared at them
and one by one they turned their eyes from him, his confusion changed to dismay. An impatient coughing, a nervous shuffling of feet, a general stir broke in upon him. His
own voice hung in the room, mocking him. "The painters
of Redmond have suffered enough laughter and ridicule
and indignity." Each word stung him like a lash. He was
the one they wanted out! What a fool he had made of
himself. He forced himself to face the audience once more.
All at once there passed from face to face a frown of indignation. It had come over them that he was to blame
for not having sensed their feelings without exposing them
to this embarrassment.

Then he suffered the most crushing realization of all. He
was not special, a solitary martyr, but only one of many
they wanted out. They lumped him with all the undesir-
ables. He raised his elbows and let them fall against his
sides. He lowered himself into his chair.

"You were wonderful, James!" Rachel whispered.

When the meeting was over they left quietly and un-
observed. A little way outside the gallery James stopped
and turned. "Give me those packages!" he said. "Are you
trying to make me look like a fool?" Rachel handed them
over and again fell two steps behind. In this way they
trudged up Main Street, around the curve and down
through town. When they passed the last house Rachel
came up and took the packages, fell back two steps, and
they walked on home.

The Ruggles had lived in each of the six shanties one

passed in going to the one they lived in now. They were
built for chicken houses. When the artists began coming
to Redmond in the 1920's an enterprising native turned
them into homes. Twenty-odd more were scattered in the
woods behind the road but only three were inhabited now
with any regularity, one by a trapper, one by a hermit and
one by the Ruggles. When one house began decaying
faster than Rachel could repair it the Ruggles moved to
another. They had been living in number seven for about
a year.

Whenever they moved Rachel got a bucket of paint and
spent weeks prettying the place. To James it seemed she
could take pride in anything. She transplanted the rose
bush and lined the path to the door with colored stones.
She straightened the palings of the fence and gave it a coat
of whitewash, while James groaned and begged her to let
him enjoy his poverty, his discomfort, instead of trying so
vainly to hide it.

On opening the door one was not in the hall or the living
room or the kitchen—he was in the house. The bedroom
and the studio were meagerly set off with screens; the
kitchen and the living room and the dining room flowed
into each other. Yet nothing seemed cramped or incon-
gruous or makeshift. One was struck by the repose of the
room, the balance of light and dark, the pleasing arrange-
ment of rich colors. Light from the windows was directed
to fall upon old-looking, rare-looking things. Softly glowing, suggestive objects rested in the shadow of the corners.
It was like stepping inside a Vermeer.

But the Hepplewhite chair was a fake. One had been
disturbed by it on first coming in. It was handsome,
though, genuine or not, so handsome that one stole further glances at it—whereupon he realized that it was never

meant to pass for a Hepplewhite. It was the Ruggles improvement on the Hepplewhite design. Then there was that small hanging glowing on one wall—it turned out to be a scrap of cloth. Still, what beautiful cloth, and who else would have dared hang it there?

When one had decided that nothing was what it seemed he found that the Persian prayer rug hanging on another wall was thick, rich, old but unfaded—genuine. The plates hanging over the mantel, then—were they genuine spode? And the Steuben glass? But by this time one no longer cared whether the things were authentic. They were real. And the realest thing was the care and taste with which they had been assembled.

Sooner or later, if one strolled about the room, he saw through a back window the outhouse, painted Chinese red, set at the edge of the woods.

It was in that bright red outhouse, ten days after the gallery meeting, that James sat thinking, "What if I were to send a picture of mine—say, *Still Life with Plaster Bust* —to Matisse? One look, and he'd see to it that I didn't stay in Redmond any longer. Or, send one to him and one to Picasso at the same time, and let them fight over the credit for discovering me."

Rachel called him in to lunch.

While he sat at the table waiting to be served he talked half to himself, half aloud. "Of course the man who would really appreciate my work is Matisse. Hmmm. What is there to lose? A package comes from America. He opens it. He is annoyed at my presumption. But he takes one look at the picture. Suppose he didn't like it?" This James asked himself, though he did not believe for a moment that it was possible. "Well, he would send it back." He thought about that for a moment, then decided that he could trust Matisse; he would send it back. "So what is there to lose?"

"Yes, what is there to lose?" asked Rachel. She was beside him, setting a plate of stew before him. "I heard you, James, and I think it's a perfectly wonderful idea. Why didn't you think of it before?"

The light died out of James's eyes. The hand with which he had been reflectively stroking his chin fell and he said, "For Christ's sake, Rachel! How can you be so childish!"

They ate silently. After lunch Rachel thought of a way to cheer him up. She said, "James, why don't we invite the David Petersons over this evening. It's been so long since I've had any company." Rachel always took upon herself any longing for company.

"What!" he roared. "Invite people to this!" He waved an open palm around the room.

Rachel ran to straighten a doily under a lamp, then the lamp shade, then a picture on the wall.

"Oh, Lord!" James moaned.

Rachel darted her eyes around the room, trying to find what else offended him. She stooped and smoothed out the rug, she adjusted a chair.

"Oh, oh, oh," James moaned.

Rachel gave up. She stood in the center of the room, her arms hanging helplessly. James gave her such a look. "You think I'm complaining about your housekeeping!" He rolled his eyes beseechingly. Then he began an elaborate exercise of self-control. "I must be charitable," he said. "I must keep in mind your background. How could you be expected to know what's wrong here? Even this is better than anything you ever knew. In fact, I expect you think you've risen quite a ways in the world. And indeed you have, you have."

So now, instead of the room, Rachel tried to straighten herself. She smoothed her hips, patted her bosom, her hair.

"Guests!" he cried. "What do you know about entertaining? You'd serve them lung stew, I suppose. But first a *vorspice*—a little *lox* maybe? Jesus! When I think of my Aunt Patience Summerfield! James Russell Lowell called her the most charming hostess in the state of Massachusetts. Not that you ever heard of him. There was a woman who knew how to entertain. What would she say to see me today? No wonder I can't get anywhere in the world! Suppose I ever did make a name for myself—could I invite anyone to this? I don't know where I get the courage to keep trying. Guests! You!"

Rachel's anguish during these harangues was not for herself but for him. She knew how tormented and disheartened he was to make him say these things. She knew James did not care one way or another about Jews. He had invented his anti-Semitism to lacerate himself.

And that was what he was doing as he tried to look scornfully at her black hair and broad cheekbones and slanted eyes. But upon her heavy breasts and wide hips his eyes began to soften, to linger. They came to rest upon her great firm thighs.

"Rachel," he said, and at once all his defenses, his anxieties, his sham fell from him, leaving him frightened, deflated, almost physically smaller, but for a moment relieved, "Rachel, without you what would ever become of me?"

"There, there," she said, rubbing her cheek against his mustache and stroking the nape of his neck, "don't you even think of it."

She helped him unbutton her, then as she unbuttoned him she smiled to think, without any spite or feeling of

193

triumph, that her Jewish looks were just what he loved—
it was, despite him, poor dear, his style of beauty.

The slight chill of the room only excited them further.

They were getting into bed when there came a knock at
the door. They looked at each other and silently agreed
to make no sound. The knock came again. Still they made
no sound. The fourth time they gave up.

Only Homer Austin could be that persistent. He knew
that the Ruggles were always at home. Besides, only Homer
ever came to see them. Only Homer could be sure to be so
ill-timed.

Homer's certainty that he would always find them there
and that he was always welcome annoyed James. Today it
infuriated him. Scantily dressed, he stood at the door with
his hands on his hips and demanded, "Who is it?"

"It's me," said the voice; the tone was: Who else?

"Who is me?"

The door opened and Homer peeped in. "I was just
passing by . . ."

"On your way to the city dump?"

Homer laughed and came in. Since no one ever seemed
glad to see him he did not notice that James was not. He
said,

"So the gallery has expelled you. Art is now the tool of
the artist class."

Homer watched eagerly for every sign of the imminent
death of art, individual freedom, human values. His mind
was filled with anticipations of persecution. He was ready
to go underground any day, though with no hope that he
would not very soon be caught and shot, or buried in a
prison. He bestowed on James Ruggles, as his friend, the
distinction of being the second victim after him of the

coming totalitarianism. Occasionally this view of him suited James's own mood.

So far as James was concerned, Homer's radicalism, indeed all radicalism, was nothing but a defense. Since Homer couldn't fit into society, he damned sure wasn't going to. But James enjoyed the flow of Homer's political jargon. He did not want to see society done over—the very notion seemed comical to him—but he loved to hear its condition criticized. As James in one of his lucid moments had said, he and Homer ate sour grapes together.

Today, however, James was in no mood to have his misfortunes treated as incidents in a general disaster.

"Of course," said Homer, beginning to relax into his chair and clasping his hands behind his head, "of course you can't blame the men personally. It's the age. They merely manifest the decay of mutual aid and the general vulgarization of taste that has followed the dissolution of the Left."

"Can't blame them personally! Listen," said James, "I'm not so broadminded as I like to seem. When I think of David Peterson with his Brooks Brothers suits and sturgeon on his table!"

"You can have all that," said Homer. "All you have to do is paint pictures that make you sick at your stomach. Of course, then you get ulcers and your sturgeon doesn't do you any good. You see, in a society like this you're beat any way you turn. Maybe you think David Peterson is a happy man? He'd change places with you in a minute."

"And Carl Robbins," said James. "Did you see that new Buick? I remember him when he didn't have a sole to his shoe. Did you see that Buick?"

"Yes, and some day he'll kill himself in it driving drunk. Not that he won't be better off. Alcoholism, ulcers, hypertension—that's the price you pay. The wages of sin. Or the wages of virtue—they get you either way."

Rachel came in from behind the screen doing her hair into a bun. With a tender look at James, she said she was going down to the mailbox.

"Well," said Homer, "let me tell you . . ."

"No," said James, "let me tell you." He got up and paced down the room and back. "Do you know why they want to get rid of me? They're afraid. The only reason for hating anybody is because you're afraid of him. And it's not me so much as what I stand for in their minds. They live in terror of anything new. They're afraid of young men coming up."

Suddenly, as he was getting his breath and about to go on, it stole over James that he had been saying that for a good while. He thought of Robbins, Peterson, Fraleigh. He had come to Redmond only a little later than they. It struck him for the first time that they were not much if any older than he; the difference was that they had arrived.

He had to sit. Homer went on talking. For the first time James began assigning the actual dates to the events of his life. He realized that 1919, 1925, even 1937 were no longer just a little while ago, no longer in the last decade. "One of the young Redmond painters," he called himself. It must have been sounding mighty foolish for quite a while now.

Gradually, without the loss of any of its poignance, the humor of it began to appeal to him. He did not mind sounding foolish so long as he was aware of it. In fact, then he enjoyed it.

"As I was saying," he brought himself back. His mustache assumed an amused tilt. "As I was saying, young men have to live, too." He waited for Homer to reveal that he saw the humor in this. Had Homer seen through him at that moment James would have been delighted with him. Homer merely arched his brows and nodded his head wearily. Homer, James decided, still thought of himself as a young man.

The door flew open and Rachel scrambled in. She caught herself up, tried to appear controlled, hoping to spring a surprise, but her excitement was too much for her. Flushed with her secret, she stood trying to build up James's suspense. But she was the one who could not stand the suspense. She thrust a letter at him. "From the Gallery," she gasped.

Hope and suspicion mingled in his face. But Rachel's certainty and enthusiasm decided him. They had changed their minds, were writing to beg his pardon. Phrases from the letter raced already through his mind: "a grievous mistake . . . a hasty faction . . . by no means representative . . . forgive any anxiety . . . an ugly misunderstanding. . . ." He had ripped open the envelope, when he stopped abruptly. He gaped at it. His face went blank, then filled with disgust. He handed the envelope slowly back to Rachel.

She stared fully a minute at it before it began to dawn on her—the letter was addressed to her. Still she could not believe it. She was sure she had read it three or four times coming back from the mailbox; it had read: "James Finley Ruggles." It seemed she had even read the letter it contained, begging James to forgive them. She gave an embarrassed little laugh. She drew out the letter.

She unfolded it and lifted out a narrow strip of yellow paper. "It's a check," she whispered. "For five hundred dollars!"

"Dear Miss Ravich, we take great pleasure in informing you that your picture *Mother and Child* has won. . . ." She stole a glance at James.

He was stunned. The thing he could not grasp was that the time had rolled around for the awarding of the prizes. He had waited, convinced each day that the Gallery Board would appear in a body to tell him that he had been accepted. He had not realized that the time was past for any possibility for that. Of course he had submitted a picture; he had never been able to believe they would really exclude him.

Rachel found herself spun around by her shoulders. "This is wonderful!" cried Homer. There were tears of joy in his eyes. "Rachel, wonderful! I'm so proud of you!"

"Yes," said James in an unsteady voice, "congratulations," and he got up and walked out of the house.

Breakfast the next morning was hardly finished when James said, "I'll do the dishes," though he did not stir from his chair.

"What!" cried Rachel. It was the last thing he might have been expected to say. Not since Rachel had known him had he ever offered to dry a cup. He scorned men who shared their women's work, and Rachel agreed with him.

"I said I'll do the dishes. I'll do all the housework from now on. It's only right. You must paint. You're a success now. You mustn't let your public down."

Rachel winced at every word. He went on, disregarding the plea on her face. "Move my easel and put yours under the north light. And use my brushes. Yours are getting pretty worn down for a famous painter." (They were pretty well worn when he passed them on to her.) "Yes, you'll have no time for housework from now on. If you keep on like this, though, maybe we can have a maid, and let me get a little painting done, just for the sake of amusement."

"I've been thinking," she said timidly, "of giving up painting altogether."

"What!" He was infuriated at her thinking her success hurt him. "Have you gone out of your mind?"

So, although he had no intention of doing the housework, he gave her no peace until she left it off. He sent her in to paint. He squeezed out her colors for her—generous gobs of each, and sat her in front of a canvas of terrifying dimensions. "Now paint!" he commanded.

Of all James Ruggles' irritations the worst had always been the notion of women painting. And more of them were taking it up every day. It was getting so any self-respecting man was ashamed to go in for it.

He went to see how Rachel's picture was coming. The canvas was blank. "You'll never get anywhere that way," he said.

By noon she still had done nothing. He gave her about ten minutes to finish her lunch, insisted that she leave the dishes and sent her back to the studio. By this time his feelings were mixed. He had come to want her to paint. Visions of the money she would bring him filled his mind. He could see himself painting all day on the Riviera, in Mexico, on some tropic island. Her painting was only woman's painting anyway. If it could bring in money for him to do serious painting then he had the laugh.

James Ruggles had strict theories on the proper way for women to paint—if paint they must. There was a time when he began to detect the influence of his own work on Rachel's. He took her to museums and stood her in front of pictures in sweet fuzzy colors of plump girls and pretty children. That, he told her, was the way for her to paint, that was woman's painting. She never doubted him; she was grateful to him for setting her right. He tried now to enjoy the irony of this, but he was forced to admit his vexation.

In the middle of the afternoon he startled her by asking how she meant to spend the money.

She came into the kitchen looking puzzled and pained. "Why, James," she said, "I hadn't thought about it. Of course there are a good many things we need. I thought we might talk it over and decide. I thought we . . ."

"We?"

"Oh, I wish I'd never seen that check!" she cried. "I'll send it back!" she whispered in a shaky voice. "I'll refuse it. We were so happy before it came. Oh, James!"

"Just think of the things you can buy yourself that I never got you," he said. "Vacuum cleaner, electric washer, television set. You could get a Persian lamb coat and look like a real *yenta*." And he went on like this all afternoon, growing more bitter and outlandish.

As they sat down to supper, "It seems to me," he said, "that this calls for a celebration. We have to throw a party."

Even in her present state of torment, the word "party" could not help but bring a smile to Rachel's lips. The storm was over, she thought; this was his way of making up. But the smile which lingered on his lips, even she could see, was unmistakably sardonic. A shudder of apprehension ran down her spine.

The first guests to arrive were the Sam Morrises. James met them at the door.

"Good evening, James!" Sam shouted.

Just to walk into the Ruggles' house was a delight for

Sam Morris. Such unconventional beauty! He stood beaming, inviting his wife to respond to the charm of the place.

Edith Morris made no effort to conceal that she had expected something very different from life as a doctor's wife from what she had got with Sam.

"Good evening, Mr. Ruggles," she said.

A smile began to play in James's mustache. "Just call me Mister Ravich," he said. Rachel was just coming from the bedroom. Her hands flew to her cheeks in horror.

Fortunately more guests arrived at that moment. Rachel led the Morrises away. The new ones whom James greeted were the John Woosters. Whether out of guilt over their share in expelling him from the gallery, or anxiety to show that they were not among those responsible, they had not dared refuse his invitation. Their discomfort inspired James with cruelty. His way of punishing them was to abase himself before them.

"So very good of you to come," he said. His tone was savagely obsequious. "Do come in," he urged.

By this time Rachel was hurrying to extricate them. When she saw who it was she grew flustered. Faye Wooster was a person she could never see without blushing. Faye used to be a model, and James had told her something simply unheard-of about Faye, something horribly funny, though it was cruel to think so. These thoughts reminded Rachel that she would also see Martha Phillips tonight. How would she manage to greet Martha, knowing all the things she now knew about her? Then there would be Carl Robbins, about whom James had told her recently. How did James manage all that coolness before these people that he knew such scandalous and personal things about?

She came to herself to hear James saying, "And please

let us not stand on ceremony. Just call me what everyone will from now on—call me Mister Ravich."

Rachel led them away.

James could not understand himself. For earlier in the day he had come actually to look forward with pleasure to the evening. He had known it would be somewhat painful to him, but he had also admitted to himself that he was lonely, and had resolved to be pleasant. He had even craftily imagined that Rachel's success might open a path to his own recognition.

Rachel flitted among the guests, keeping them talking and laughing. James stayed at the door. The face of each new guest filled him with loathing and anger. Rachel ran to greet each new arrival, but not before James had managed to shout to him that he was to be addressed as Mister Ravich. The room filled and the talk grew louder, louder still as the guests, out of their mounting embarrassment and indignation, tried to drown out his shameless, painful joke. But he managed to make himself heard each time.

Finally he gave up his station at the door to join the party. He came examining the face of each guest, anxious to find one of them revealing that he had come out of pity, or for amusement, or that he was feeling uncomfortable.

But everyone was enjoying himself quite innocently. Sixteen guests had come. The John Woosters clung together, and Mrs. Wooster regarded James with apprehension. Edith Morris had a corner of the divan to herself, much to her satisfaction. But everyone else was gay. The David Petersons had come and James remarked that Dolly had not seen fit to wear her silver fox stole or one of her Paris originals. Max Aronson was there and had lost all his usual nervousness. Max was known to feel that people who had just had good news were happier to see him, being then no longer quite so envious of him. But his joy in someone else's good fortune was as great as in his own, so he hovered over Rachel in a perfect dither of happiness.

Martha Phillips had shown up, bringing with her a visitor, Mrs. Kunitz, who had been better known in Redmond as Muriel Johnson, but who corrected no one's calling her Mrs. Kunitz. For Mrs. Kunitz, then, it was old home week. She once lived next to the Ruggles and never bothered pulling down her shade at night. In those days she always looked as though she had just got up—eyes puffy and ringed, hair blowzy. Obviously it had been meant to show that she was too taken up with her art to bother. She even won some kind of prize, James seemed to recall. She had quite suddenly married Mr. Kunitz, a widower in wholesale groceries, who was in Redmond for a vacation, and a cure, ten years ago. Now she was greatly amused at the distance she had come. It seemed to astound her afresh each moment that people still lived like this, still took seriously the things these people did.

As was his way at gatherings, Carl Robbins had abandoned his wife the moment they came in, and though the room was small he managed to keep a great deal of distance between them. She was pregnant with her third effort to keep Carl at home. The evening had turned off warm, the windows were up and Carl Robbins, like everyone else, was helping himself plentifully to the beer.

Despite himself, James felt beginning to steal over him a warm satisfaction at being a host, having people drink and laugh and enjoy themselves in his house. Rachel's spicy little liver knishes were a great success, they brought tears to Max Aronson's eyes and set him reminiscing over the famous cooks in his family, and when they were gone Rachel suggested games.

Games? Two or three of the guests exchanged significant glances. What were they in for now?

"Or, David," Rachel said, "give some of your impersonations!"

Peterson flushed and looked sheepishly at his wife. Dolly had got him—how many years ago!—to give up making a fool of himself in public. He felt guilty also that it showed how long it was since he had been friendly with the Ruggles. No one had reminded him of his impersonations in years. And yet, he thought, with a look of some defiance at his wife, they were damned clever impersonations. Especially the one of Chaplin (but again, how long ago was Chaplin!) and he was pleased with Rachel for remembering them. All the same he demurred; he, too, thought that impersonations were no longer becoming to his dignity. Besides, no one was coaxing him but Rachel. And besides, Dolly's look was quite threatening.

"Then let's play games," Rachel insisted. She supposed that games were no longer quite so popular at Redmond parties, but she wanted to revive some of the spirit of parties she remembered.

"What sort of games?" asked John Wooster.

"A community picture!" Rachel cried, and ran off to the studio where they heard her scrambling about.

How long was it since any of them had painted a community picture! In the old days it was a party stand-by. Now the ladies exchanged smiles of pity and condescension for poor Rachel. How long it must have been since she had given a party! How much longer even since she had been invited to one, not to know that community pictures were *passé*.

Rachel came back bearing the easel and on it was a large

204

canvas. She made another trip for brushes and a palette and all was placed in the middle of the room.

No one would go first.

"Then I'll choose," said Rachel. "And David is it, since he wouldn't give us any impersonations."

She handed Peterson a fistful of brushes and led him to the easel. Everyone enjoyed his discomfort.

But Peterson was a good sport. He regarded the canvas, took a few tentative swipes at it, then began wielding the brush with dash, with obvious relish. Vague, but already recognizable and already funny forms began to take shape on the canvas. For everyone knew what he had to put there before he began. In painting a community picture each person contributed the little mark of his style, his *petit sensation*, the little mannerism or the subject by which his work was known. Soon it became apparent that David Peterson was doing one of those hollow-eyed, nebulous nudes for which he was famous, but one even more gaunt and soulful—a delightful self-parody. Peterson had been taken right back ten years and was having a marvelous time.

Peterson stepped back to regard his creation and everyone was hugely amused. There was no lack of volunteers for second; they fought to be next, and Rachel had to choose to keep order.

Max Aronson started in a little above and to the left of Peterson's lady and from his first stroke everyone began laughing uncontrollably. In no time at all there took form one of those bleary-eyed, long-faced, ancient rabbis for which Max was known all over the world—only this rabbi, while looking just as burdened with *Weltschmerz* as ever, even more ludicrously so, was regarding Peterson's lady with a sly and lecherous glint in his eye. Everyone held his sides laughing.

Then Carl Robbins and Martha Phillips took brushes and began painting at the same time, racing each other while everyone cheered them on.

At this point Mrs. Kunitz drained her beer glass and set it down, looked searchingly into every corner of the house, got up and peered around the studio screen, and still not finding what she wanted, came over and bent to Rachel's ear.

"You'll find it," said James in a voice that made everyone hush and turn, "about thirty yards behind the house. Just follow your nose. Would you have believed it possible in this day and age?"

They were pressing Rachel to add her bit to the painting. "Get James," she said, "get James." The tone of his voice had alarmed her, and she breathed a sigh of relief for this distraction.

"Here, James," said Carl Robbins, holding out a brush to him.

James made no move, but left Robbins standing, awkwardly holding out the brush. The others stirred uneasily. James raised his palm in a gesture of overwhelmed unworthiness. "Let me not bring laughter and ridicule and indignity to this work," he said. A hush fell on them all.

But on her whole trip nothing had so delighted Mrs. Kunitz as the outhouse. "Well! That's the first time I've seen one of those things in a while!" she said as she stepped in.

"Yes, we keep it for sentimental reasons," said James. "Not to mention other reasons." The prolonged, stunned silence of the guests made him more audacious. "We try to keep up the old traditions. People come expecting to see the real thing, the artist's life, you know—and where else are they going to find it in Redmond? Though now," and he gave a glance at Rachel, a deferential smile, "now I suppose we too will begin to slip and backslide and forget the simple life. In fact," his voice rose to a shout, "in fact, we have already begun. Indeed yes!"

He relished their embarrassment for a moment, then said, "I'm sure you're all dying to know what's been done with the money. Well, let me just show you. None of you is quite as, ah, thin, as you once were. But just draw in a breath and perhaps we can all squeeze into the, ah, the bedroom."

He strode over and folded back the bedroom screen with a flourish.

"There!" he exclaimed. "Our prize money bedroom suite!"

The little room looked positively embarrassed. In it stood a huge highboy, a vanity with an oval mirror tinted blue, a padded vanity seat covered with glossy satin and a bed with a gleaming headboard, covered with a bright blue chenille spread.

The silence was broken by the ladies' exclamations. "Lovely. Charming. How nice." The men assented in embarrassed grunts.

Rachel had seen it yesterday in the window of a shop in Redmond, where she had gone to get away from James and to look for something to get rid of the money on. Her mother had had one very like it. Rachel thought it was beautiful.

How was it, then, that otherwise the house was so tasteful? Was that all James's doing? Far from it. In fact, aside from his contribution of a few heirlooms—some of them among the few ugly things in the house—he had no part in it. He was indifferent to his surroundings. So long as they could not come up to his notions of what they should be, he preferred to go to the opposite extreme; it would have given him pleasure to live off orange crates and hang dime-store chromos on the walls. No, the charm of the place was Rachel's doing. But Rachel had taste only so long as she had no money. When her resourcefulness was demanded, when she had to make shift, she made beauty. When she had money she bought the things she thought other people bought with money, the things she remembered money as being for.

"Lovely, isn't it?" James demanded of Mrs. Wooster.

"Yes—yes, lovely!" and she cringed against her husband.

"Isn't it lovely?" he shouted at Edith Morris.

"It certainly is," said Edith. She meant it.

James included them both in his look of utter contempt. "Maple, you know," he said, looking at the furniture with nausea. "That is, pine with a coat of maple syrup."

Those who were not too embarrassed for Rachel even to look at her, sent her looks of sympathy and support. John Wooster said, "We had better go."

James was taken aback. "Go?" he said. He had humiliated himself for them. Weren't they enjoying it?

The Woosters began moving toward the door; others followed. James saw all his crafty plans collapsing. He grew panicky to keep them there. His urgency gave a repulsive oiliness to his smile and the affability of his tone was repellent as he said, "Come now. You're all used to staying up later than this. The evening's young." He realized he was saying the wrong thing. This pleased him and goaded him on. "Why, there's no telling what may happen yet," he said.

He stood in the middle of the room and watched them

leave. He half-expected them to return, to slap him on the back and say that he was better than all of them put together. He could think of nothing startling to say, no show to make which would detain them. He wanted to say something disdainful, something contemptible even, yet have them admire him all the more for it.

The last ones were stepping out. James thought how as they walked down the road Sam Morris would take it upon himself to explain him to the rest. "It's James's nature," he would say knowingly, "to be volatile and impulsive, always to be different and conspicuous." Sam was certain he understood James. How James hated that kind of understanding! For if he acted extravagantly, made himself conspicuous, it was all because he had such a great wish to do just the opposite, because he had such great respect for convention and the proper form.

Rachel stepped outside and detained the last few. "James doesn't mean anything by it when he goes off like that," she said in an intimate tone. "You needn't feel sorry for me, because he is always terribly sorry afterwards. It's only his own unhappiness."

They gaped at her. Was she then as bad as he? Had she no more sense of privacy than he had? It was shameless, such confiding eagerness.

Not all the prize money was spent on the bedroom suite. Thirty-six dollars went for the suit in which James stood admiring himself on a morning two weeks after the party. It was the first one the clerk had shown him, and he had liked it right off. When he tried it on at home he found the pinstripe too broad and too light in color, but that no longer bothered him. He stroked the lapel lovingly.

Another seven dollars went for the shoes.

James turned and looked at himself from the back, particularly at his haircut. Then he faced himself once more and looked at his mustache. His mustache had been clipped and trimmed and his curls lopped off so that now his hair lay in tight kinks against his skull.

He wore a white shirt with a starched collar so cruelly buttoned that his great red neck hung over it in a roll, and after swallowing he had to duck his head to get his Adam's apple up again.

Every few seconds he was worried that the suit was not what it should be. It had been so long since he had bought one. Then he would again decide that it was grand.

The thing which amazed and delighted him most was that he looked just like anybody else. He might be in advertising or the law.

Rachel came in rubbing the crown of a new brown hat with her elbow. But when he put it on it fell down over his ears. He had bought it before Rachel cut his hair. She took the blame for that, but said that a little tissue paper in the sweatband would fix it.

While she went to get some, James polished the emblem in his lapel and pictured himself at the fraternity house tomorrow evening after the Reunion Dinner. He was amazed that he had gone so many years without attending Reunion Day. He saw himself sitting back in his chair with his legs crossed, sipping Benedictine while he talked with Pee-wee Moore, now Charles Moore of Ohio, Michigan, Ltd. or with Walter Beck of U. S. Steel.

Men like Moore and Beck would, of course, know nothing of the art world. But they would simply assume that he had done well. Especially when they saw him in this suit. He looked at it again to be sure, and he decided once and for all that it was not so much what the suit did for him, as what he did for the suit.

Besides Beck and Moore there were men like Joseph Caspar and William Malcolm Cooper in the class of '26. That was his class. Or rather, the class he would have been in if he had stayed another year.

"Rachel," he said, "these men I'm going to be with the next couple of days are my kind of people. They come from the best families. They were brought up to respect ceremony and tradition. They know what culture is. And don't think they won't remember me. They know what the name Ruggles means."

The taxi that was to take him to the train pulled up outside the door and honked.

Rachel carried out his grip and the bundle of paintings. He had decided first to take five, then eight; now there were eleven of them and it was arranged that Rachel was to send ten more tomorrow by express.

He looked at them and smiled shrewdly.

"I can ask any price from men like those," he said. "What's money to them?"

A Fresh Snow

~~~~~~

It was silly and a waste of time. School was not
even out yet. She could not expect him for half
an hour at least. Still she sat at the window watching the
corner of the block.

Snow, dingy with soot, lay thick upon the window ledge.
The street ran with slush and through the gray light hov-
ering in the street the mass of buildings opposite looked
black and close.

As she watched, a few large flakes began to fall. They
lighted on the window ledge, and bending forward to
look at them, her breath condensing on the glass, she
thought of the thrilling, rare snows of her childhood.

She had been five years old when she was wakened in
the night to see her first snow. Wrapped in quilts, she
and her brother had stood at the window wiping away the
steam of their breaths and peering into the blackness,
while their father told of the snows he had seen. Two
inches fell that night, a good fall, and in the morning the
grownups were gay and happy for the children's sake. After
breakfast everyone went out with soupbowls. Each looked
for a drifted spot to fill his bowl; even so, they had to
scrape lightly to keep from picking up dirt. They ate it

sprinkled with sugar and flavored with vanilla extract. Her brother came home in midmorning, for school had been let out to celebrate, and through the afternoon they watched the snow disappear. By night it was gone. She was eight before she saw her next.

Otherwise the winters there were fitful times, days of pale sun followed by days of slashing rain. How often she had sat looking out at the dripping trees and the colorless, sodden fields. Seven years before she had sat all day for weeks at the parlor window in her brother Leon's house. Then she was waiting for Donald to be born. Leon had taken her in when she grew too big to work in the confectionery or climb the three flights of the boarding house in town. She had had to stay behind when George was transferred from the camp. There was no housing in California and George was expecting to go overseas any day. Donald was three years old before his father saw him.

She had met George in the confectionery where she was the cashier. The soldiers from the camp were mostly Northern boys and the town mistrusted girls who went out with them. She always rang up their bills and counted out their change with a quickness which discouraged conversation. But George never tried to say more than "thank you." Perhaps it piqued her that her distance suited him that well. In time he grew friendly and she did not remember his former silence against him. One thing right off stood in his favor: he was not an officer. She mistrusted even Southerners who were officers. And once you got to know him George turned out to be a regular tease. She had always enjoyed being gently teased, and when George mimicked her accent, saying, "Yawl fetch it an Ah hep ye tote it," she felt she was being appreciated in a pleasant new way. He teased her also with outlandish tales about

214

the North, but she was more impressed when he told her the truth, such as when he described the bolt factory where he worked, which employed more men on each shift than there were in her countyseat. She began to compare him to the local boys whom she knew she might at times have had, and she was glad she had done nothing hasty. To have been forced to settle down with never a glimpse of the world beyond came to seem a dreary life.

What foolish notions she had formed then, and how long ago it seemed. Now she was a regular city dweller. If her kinfolks could see her would they think she was much changed?

A sudden darkening of the light made her turn to the window. The snow was thickening. Down in the street an old bent man was groping along. He was pulling a child's sled on which rode a small carton of groceries. His rapid breath condensed in feeble whiffs and he swayed a little from side to side.

Cities, as she had thought so many times, were no place for old folks. No one had time to help or notice them. Whenever she saw an old man waiting helplessly on a street corner or risking the traffic she was thankful that her poor father had lived and died down South. She was glad she had been with him that last year, glad that he had lived to see Donald and glad she had let him believe that when George came back they were going to settle on the old homeplace. He had liked George. He liked a man, no matter where he was from, who looked you square in the eye, who put something into his handshake, who was not a damned smart aleck. Of course he had felt bound to say something about the Civil War. She remembered well his surprise and her own when George said he did not know whether any of his ancestors had fought in it.

She closed her eyes and saw her father's grave lying under a steady gray rain. She could see the whole family plot and she named them off in order in her mind, with their dates and epitaphs. Another month and it would be graveyard-cleaning time. Surely that old custom had not died out since she went away. It had been such a good time for all, a little melancholy, but not solemn, as you might think. Everyone came early bringing garden rakes and worn-down brooms. It would be the first nice day in spring, still cool enough to work comfortably and make it pleasant to smell the fires of rotted leaves. The children ran and played, being careful not to tread on any graves, of course. It was not thought good taste to clean the graves of your own kin. You cleaned other people's plots and trusted them to clean yours. The children's special chore was to clean and decorate the graves of little children. Each brought a "pretty"—something weatherproof—a china doll or a glass doorknob or a colored bottle, and with these they decorated the graves while they told again the sweetly sad story of each dead child. Then came dinner on the ground. Each woman brought the dish she was famous for and everybody knew without asking whom to compliment on each dish. Her mother always brought pecan pie. It was a time known for forming friendships among the children and courtships among the young. By night the graves had been raked and swept and the headstones straightened, and by then all the men had gone a few times out to the woods where a bottle was kept, so everyone went home feeling tired and happy, pleasantly melancholy, and good friends with the whole community. It seemed you were born knowing the names of every member of every family and when they were born and died, and after a while it came to seem that you had known them all per-

216

sonally all your life and their loss was a personal loss to you.

Often she had wondered where the city dead were buried and how they were looked after, but a feeling of propriety came over her and she hesitated to ask. Surely they could not be as forgotten as they seemed to be. In George's family they never mentioned their dead. You would think they had no kin beyond the living ones.

She saw in her mind the unfinished stone beside her father's grave. It could not be long before her mother would lie there. Would she see her again before that time? What would the date read on that stone? Donald seemed to be losing his memory of his grandmother. Would he see her once more so he could have a memory of her? George would have let her have her mother with her, but her mother would not come. It was just as well, she supposed. It pained her to think how helpless and out of place and lonely her mother would feel, cut off from her old ways, her relatives and old friends. She would feel so lost and frightened, caught in the shrill, jostling store crowds. She would have sorrowed all day to have been yelled at by the butcher in the chain store.

"Mek up yer mind, lady, mek up yer mind!"

Would her mother find her much changed? She had tried to be a good wife to George. She had believed she ought to try to forget the ways she had been brought up to when they were different from her husband's ways. But there were things she felt she would never get used to. She remembered George's mother asking her right off what nationality she was. If you asked anybody that question back home then you were already sure he was some kind of foreigner, and beneath taking exception.

She looked out for some sight of Donald, but the street

was empty. She lay back in her chair and saw herself and him stepping out of the bus in the depot back home. Should she let them know she was coming, or surprise them? If she wrote ahead they would go to a lot of trouble, but, she must admit, that would not have displeased her. They would exclaim over Donald and disagree about which person in the family he looked most like. Strange to realize that many things, so familiar to her, would have to be explained to Donald. In the afternoon they would have people over, relatives and old friends, to sit on the porch and talk. They would tell of births and deaths and talk of the weather and crops, of the things they had always talked about, of life and the afterlife, and stretched out in the porch swing she would feel herself soothed by the warm breeze and by the slow warm liquid flow of Southern voices.

She was startled from her thoughts by the sound of running on the stairs. She had forgotten what she was waiting for and for a moment the sight of the boy in the door awoke no memory in her. She looked at him without recognition. He wore thick snow pants and a padded jacket, heavy rubber boots and a fur cap with large muffs from which his face peeped out red with cold. He was covered with snow. He had dashed in so quickly from outside that flakes still clung to his cheeks and in his brows and lashes.

He closed the door and stamped in, shaking himself like a dog and giving off the smell of cold wool and cold rubber. When he neared her she felt the cold which surrounded him and it seemed to penetrate to her heart. She stood up in an impulse of fear.

"I gotta get my sled. Me and a gang of boys are going to the park," he said. "They're meeting me on the corner in five minutes."

Even his voice seemed stiff with cold. What kind of talk was that, so sharp and nasal? That was not the voice she had given him! She heard the voice of her kin reproach her for bringing up her son in forgetfulness of them.

"No," she cried. "You can't go. Stay with me."

Her strangeness frightened him. He said weakly, "But I told them I would. They've all gone to get their sleds."

But she would not let him go. She made him take off his things. She put cocoa on the range to heat and when it was done she sat him on her lap and rocked him softly, his head against her breast, while she told him all about the South, where he was born.

The Hardys

~~~~~~

Mr. Hardy sat on the edge of the bed waiting
for his mind to catch up, and told himself
that today he ought to be especially nice to Clara.

He reached for his twist on the nightstand and, marking
the spot with his thumb, carefully measured off his morning chew. He wrapped his teeth around it, then decided it
wasn't quite what he needed and wrung off a man-sized
plug. He gathered his clothes from the chair. In his sock
feet, gaiters in his hand, he paused at the door and listened;
Clara slept soundly.

Holding a kidney in place, Mr. Hardy bent to light the
stove. He spat in the ash box and stashed his quid in the
corner of his mouth so he could blow the fire. He set the
coffeepot on the lid and put the biscuits in the oven and
thought there was time to look the place over a bit before
they started in on it, maybe tuck a few old things out of
sight that Clara would cry over if she came across them.

The loose floor board just inside the dining room sighed
under Mr. Hardy's feet. For the first time in he didn't
know how long, he thought of Virgie. She was worn out
from her trip, a new bride, new to Texas and scared, but
trying to be brave and trying not to show how ugly and

ramshackle this house seemed to her, and he said he would get to that board the very next morning.

When he rummaged around in his mind for a picture of her, Mr. Hardy found that Virgie's face and Clara's, like two old tintypes laid face to face in an album, had come off on each other. What would Virgie have come to look like, he wondered, if she had lived? The only way he could picture her was about like Clara looked now. The main thing Mr. Hardy recalled about his first wife was that she died and he married Clara. The three years that lay between had been lost in the shuffle. Mr. Hardy could thumb through his years like pages in a book, but looking up a certain one was like hunting a sentence he had come across years before. "How was it, Mr. Hardy, you took so long about getting married again?" he could remember Clara asking more than once, and of course he answered, "I was a while finding the right woman." It seemed now he hardly waited a decent time after laying Virgie in the ground. Being without a wife had made him feel queer. With three stepchildren to take on, and all boys so she couldn't expect any help with the housework, he was afraid no woman would have him. At the same time he feared some other man might see the day's work Clara Dodson could do and grab her up, she might just be waiting for a chance to lay down, he suspected, when she was mistress of a house of her own.

He needn't have worried about Clara, Mr. Hardy told himself, feeling guilty for standing off and thinking about her in such a cold-hearted way. As long as she was able she worked night and day, and often he wondered if even Virgie could have made a better mother to her boys.

Little by little, as Virgie's belongings got shoved further back in the attic of the house, Virgie had been pushed further and further back in the unused corners of Mr. Hardy's mind. He all but forgot they were Virgie's children, that this had ever been any but Clara's house.

Mrs. Hardy woke up just in time. Breathless, she lay listening to the thump of her heart, sure she had barely missed being taken, and thinking over what a terrible night she had been through. For each time she woke Mr. Hardy to rub her, there were ten times, she thought, when she bore her pain alone and in silence. If only Mr. Hardy would stay awake and talk to her a little while in bed at night. She would have rested ever so much better. Lying there in the quiet with her teeth out unnerved her, made her less certain of things, brought on bad dreams.

Each morning she felt glad all over again that never in thirty years had she once let Mr. Hardy see her with her teeth out. She trusted him not to look when he got up in the morning, and when she had to wake him she always took them from the tumbler first and eased them in. She smiled, thinking how Mr. Hardy always waited then, fumbling around as if he couldn't find the matches—in his own mind giving her a minute to wrap herself modestly—before lighting the lamp.

Mr. Hardy was nice in little ways like that, considerate, not like other men at all, and she ought not to complain if he was so quiet. Men just had little to say. She was used to all kinds, all funny in their own ways and no two alike except in one thing—men just never had much to say, and anything she couldn't put up with was one that did, you couldn't put any trust in them; she had never been much of a talker herself and couldn't stand gabbing women— still, being alone together as they were now, she did wish Mr. Hardy would try to be a little more company to her.

At least when he did find something to say it wasn't like other men, like the husbands of every other woman she could call to mind without exception, something sour-tempered or coarse, as if they begrudged you every word.

Being considerate by nature, Mr. Hardy would have opened out more, she felt, if he had been an American. But the English were close-mouthed and, to tell the truth, a little slow, she had long ago decided. Being English explained a lot of Mr. Hardy's quirks. Many times she had to make amends for his blunt manners to people he never really meant to hurt at all. He saved in niggling little ways. Nobody liked to see waste, but Mr. Hardy took it too far altogether.

It was being English had made him always work so hard, harder than he had to and harder than he need have let the neighbors pass by and see him at. There was nobody to blame but himself that now in his old age he had to sell his home; he had worked all the boys so hard it was no wonder each of them had enough farming by the time he was grown to last him the rest of his life.

Walking quietly, Mr. Hardy looked over the parlor until he saw on the mantelpiece the price tags the auctioneer had left. For weeks Clara had been telling everybody about the sale. She wanted them all to be sure it was not for money, but only because the house was too big, "now that the boys were all gone away," she said with pride, for she thought they had all come up in the world by moving into town. If there was anything that could come over him sometimes and make him feel he couldn't hold his head up before the neighbors, that was it.

It was terrible to have put in fifty years' hard work on a place and raised eight boys on it and there be not one among them willing to take up when you had done all you could and put in an honest day's work to keep it in the family. A great big bunch of conniving schemers with pasty-faced, shifty-eyed youngsters growing up just like them or worse. City slickers, that was what he had raised and whose bread he would have to eat from now on.

Clara, he expected, was looking forward to leaving, and he couldn't really blame her. It was a big house, and though they used little of it, hard to keep up. The very idea of a colored woman coming in to do the cleaning, handling all her stuff and dropping and breaking things, was enough to bring on one of her attacks. She would enjoy moving from one of the children to another in the time left them and he supposed that was how it would be. For a while he told himself they might take what money the old place brought and buy a little one with a couple of rooms and garden space, but Clara would never be happy in it, she would be mortified before the neighbors. A woman would rather have no home of her own at all than one without a big parlor with a sofa in it, and he had known all along it wouldn't turn out the way he wanted. A time came when you were too old for starting over.

Mrs. Hardy came into the kitchen rubbing her eyes and smelled the biscuits burning. She was in time, but if they had been burnt to a crisp, the idea of Mr. Hardy thinking to get breakfast would have made up for it. She thought of the day that lay ahead of her and how all sad things bring a little sweet with the bitter. Waiting for the eggs to boil she wondered what Mr. Hardy found so interesting he forgot about the biscuits. He was always mindful of such things, forever saying, "Now, Clara, don't forget about the biscuits," when to be sure she had forgot, her mind a thousand miles away.

When the eggs were done and still Mr. Hardy didn't come, she began to fidget. There were things about this day she had been dreading for weeks, and now she hoped he hadn't stumbled across a reminder of some old sadness and she not by his side to comfort him. Most such things had been done away with as she gradually made life easier for him, but some few, she always feared, might still be lying about.

She listened for his step in the attic. Could Mr. Hardy be sitting up there going through that box of Virgie's old things, too engrossed to stir?

He came in from outside, looking a little sheepish, it seemed to her. He had let the biscuits burn, she told him, and waited for him to say where he had been. She ought to try to get a bite down, he said, but the idea of food simply gagged her. Mr. Hardy felt he was not showing his own sense of the sadness of this day and pushed his plate back, but she said just because she couldn't eat he mustn't let that stop him.

She sighed and said she didn't know where to begin. It made no difference as far as he could see. He dug a pencil stub out of the silverware drawer. In the parlor they tried to choose what to hang the first tag on. She would have started in on little things and gradually got herself used to the idea, but Mr. Hardy went straight over to the player piano, the biggest thing in the room and the one over which she would have hesitated longest. Mr. Hardy stepped back and looked at it and thought it made the piano look suddenly very important. He imagined the auctioneer going through his spiel, "Now what am I bid for this fine player piano?" the bids going higher and higher, being called in from the front yard where the crowd had overflowed. He was beginning to enjoy himself.

"That player piano," said Mrs. Hardy, beginning to feel he was parting with it a bit too readily, "has been like a close friend to me. Many a night I believe I'd have went out of my mind if it hadn't been for that player piano."

"Well, maybe we could keep it," he said. "Isabel could find a place for it, I suppose, and you could listen to it whenever we went to stay with her."

She could listen to it; it meant nothing to him, all those fine old tunes she thought had stood for so much between them. No, she told him, they mustn't hang back over the first piece, they'd never raise any money. Well, now, they weren't that bad off; if she wanted it she would have it.

Mr. Hardy could not remember what he had paid for it and thought Clara was high when she insisted on a hundred dollars. Anyhow, they had used it a long time. Yes, but it was like new when they got it. They put down fifty dollars as the least they would take for it, and a note saying he could come down to $37.50 if that was all he could get; then Clara said to put down he ought to try to get fifty though, for it had the finest tone of any she ever heard. She stroked it. For one last time she wanted to hear *Over the Waves* and asked if he wouldn't like to, too. Really he thought they ought to get on, but he knew that tune meant a great deal to her.

She could close her eyes and hear it in her head any hour of the day and it was the night of her wedding when Mr. Hardy waltzed her till two o'clock in the morning. To look at him now who would ever believe it?

She hummed and swayed her head and tapped her foot and smiled to think she hadn't had two dozen words with Mr. Hardy when he asked her to marry him. No denying, he needed somebody to look after his boys, but there were others that he must have seen would do for that job just as well. At first she feared the change. But there was so little difference she felt at home right away, looking after Mr. Hardy and his boys instead of her father and brother and sister. For six months there was hardly time to think of anything; without a woman for three years the house, the boys, their shirts and socks all needed mending and darning, scrubbing and barbering. He told her to ease up a little, that she would kill herself with work as his first wife, Virgie, had done. No one had ever worried before how long or hard she worked. She had loved her mother and father, her brother and sister, but she grew to love Mr. Hardy so much more than all of them it made her ashamed. She came to think it had been sinful of her to marry him without feeling then as she did now about him. She thought of Virgie and dug out an old picture of her and, gazing at it, spent hours wondering if she had felt that way, too, about Mr. Hardy, which loved him the most, thinking up things she would do for him that Virgie, you could tell by her face, would have fallen short of.

The music stopped. If only there had been someone to pump the machine she would have asked Mr. Hardy to waltz with her, she was sure she still remembered the steps. He seemed impatient and she just wondered if he had forgot what tune that was.

When they were agreed on the davenport and the Morris chair, the marble-topped table and the chandelier, Mrs. Hardy took the photograph album, the mantelpiece clock, a couple of antimacassars her mother had crocheted, two or three pieces off the whatnot, and the music roll for *Over the Waves* and went out to look at the buffet while it still had no price tag on it. She had tried for days to figure out some way of keeping it, but it was just too big. She could already see Cora Westfall going straight through the rest of the house until she came to that buffet; the woman had envied her that piece for years. Mrs. Hardy only hoped somebody else turned up who wanted it as bad and ran the bid up good and high.

She watched Mr. Hardy and the way he was putting that tag on the bedroom chiffonier anybody might have thought it was just any old thing instead of the present from the children on their twenty-fifth anniversary. Men never put much store in things, she knew, but that had not stopped her from hoping Mr. Hardy might be different. He never kept souvenirs. "Souvenir of what?" she could remember him asking at the end of days she would never forget as long as she lived. She must have a keepsake for everything that ever happened to her. She had come across a good many that no longer reminded her of whatever they were supposed to. All the same they meant a great deal to her. It would all come back to her in time.

By eleven o'clock Mrs. Hardy was tired, but he was the first to notice. He settled her with a pillow behind her head to rest in the Morris chair, but not before he had removed the price tag, for she said it made her feel she was up on the auction block. She eased herself 'out with a sigh and thought that even Mr. Hardy's attentions could sometimes cause her pain. He was tender with her, when he thought about it. He ought to know he could call on her to bear the sadness with him, that he needn't try to spare her any of it. Perhaps he was worrying what the neighbors might be saying, that he had failed her, left her without a home of her own in her last years. She didn't want anybody to hold anything against him on her account.

She was watching Mr. Hardy through the open door but turned her head so as not to see the trouble he was having getting up off his knees. She had had the best years of his life, she told herself. He had grown old by her side. But he had never been young by it and that was the thing she couldn't bear to think about. She said: A man's second choice was made when he knew better what he wanted, when he knew from experience what to steer clear of, when he looked deeper than a pretty face. It was only with a ripeness of years, as everybody knew, that true love came.

But as he worked he handled more carefully the things that had been Virgie's, held them longer in his hands as though he hated to give them up. A guilty feeling would come over him and what was it worth if he was gentle with her *then?* Watching him ponder over a lamp that had been brought out for Virgie all the way from St. Louis, then break off suddenly to come in and pat her head and say a word, she felt she was getting only the crumbs that fell from the table. Such a rush of old feeling for Virgie had risen in him, he would have said a loving word to anybody that stood near.

Mr. Hardy's little niceties were the only way he knew how to behave. She couldn't remember ever having seen him lose his temper. But so with Virgie, too, he must have been sweet and good and kind. She didn't enjoy thinking he had got on exactly badly with his first wife. In her own sure ways she had made life easier for him, but it hurt her to think he had ever been really unhappy. She hoped he hadn't stayed a widower for three years only because his first marriage had been unfortunate.

Sitting alone a feeling came over her that her whole life had been an accident. What if Virgie hadn't died? But she did and Mr. Hardy chose her, after looking the field over for a long time.

230

Mr. Hardy crossed the silver on his plate and tilted his chair back, feeling he ought to say something. He saw in a corner the pile of things Clara meant to keep from the sale. They had only been over the bottom part of the house and already she could start a rag and bone shop with the stuff she had put aside. He could ransack the rest of it, a suspicion came over Mr. Hardy, and not find in this house a single thing that was really his and his alone. Clara had so many things and got such enjoyment from each of them. He found a sixpence, worn smooth, and a rusty penknife from Sheffield; they were his and they were about all.

Clara had to stop and reminisce over everything she came across and persuade herself to part with it. If the job was ever to get done they ought to separate for the rest of the day. But he could not trust her to put sensible prices on things. Already he had spent a good half-hour talking her, first into giving it up at all, then out of asking five dollars for an old table that was not worth fifteen cents and ought, in fact, to have been chopped into kindling long ago, but was the one, she maintained, on which she had fixed the first meal she ever made for him. Then, things that were in perfectly good shape, unless they had some memory for her, she was liable to let go for nothing.

He struck a bargain with her—she could sort the things in the children's rooms if she would leave the rest of the house to him. How nice it would have been, she sighed, to go around with him and recall old times together as they turned up things, but as he didn't want her, she agreed. She worked her way up the steps and when she got her breath back, found she could not get up for the load of memories the girls' room laid on her.

If there was such a thing as being sorry and glad about

something at the same time, thought Mrs. Hardy, she felt that way about leaving the house. Really her life hadn't been lived at all the way it was meant to be. It was a mistake to spend your life doing the same things day after day and she never got over feeling she was meant for something better, exactly what, she couldn't say, but she felt she would have been a great one for change, for setting out on new things, traveling. You could change the furniture around every week but it still all had to be dusted.

The trouble was, when a change happened to her it never really made much difference. Even the auction sale and leaving the home she had known so long she could barely remember any other, no longer seemed such a great upheaval, in fact, seemed already done with, accustomed to. Now, instead of her own, she would have a steady succession of her children's houses to look after, their children to bring up, just the same old thing when you got right down to it. It must be wonderful to look ahead and find in the days coming up a choice of ways to spend them. There were only the same old ways of doing the same old things, so she always fell back on the past; what else was there to think about?

She liked to sit like this and figure up how many diapers she must have washed in her time, how many times she had scrubbed this floor, how many strokes she had taken on the churn, and as the numbers climbed beyond her reckoning, she would sit back and rock inside herself in contented amazement. She liked best of all to recall suddenly that she had borne Mr. Hardy ten children.

Pregnancy had taken her by surprise. Mr. Hardy had to tell her she was in the family way. Her ignorance touched him. He thought it becoming; the truth was, as near as she could guess, it had not occurred to her. She had raised so many children not hers, children who had never known their own mothers, beginning at home with her brother and sister, then two cousins and then Mr. Hardy's boys, maybe she had forgot that children could have mothers of their own, that living women might have children.

Taken by surprise, she hadn't enjoyed that first confinement much, Mrs. Hardy thought. She had been scared. There was no time to store up memories of it, not time even to think up a name for the child, only time to think that if it was a boy she couldn't name it Charles Junior and, despite all she could do, to get to disliking the little boy who already bore that name through no fault of his own. The sickness and the pain she remembered and, as though it was yesterday, the feeling that came over her when they laid the child, raw and red, in her arms and she remembered that this was not new to Mr. Hardy, that he had gone through it for the first time with someone else. The doctor smiled and said she would be all right. She thought of how the other woman had gone through all this twice for Mr. Hardy and trying once again, died at it for him.

She made up her mind to live for Mr. Hardy. Out of bed a week her joy in the child grew such that she determined to have another as soon as possible. For twenty years she was never happy unless she was with child or brought to bed of one.

She had her favorites but didn't show it. Mr. Hardy had none and that had always made her feel he didn't like any of them well enough. He made a little joke, that, to be frank, she never had found so funny, of telling the children she was never pleased with any of them and would keep on having more until she was. Her pains were severe. She loved them all and the more she had the more she loved Virgie's as well, but her own she never forgave the travail they cost her coming into the world. "Lord!" she could gasp at one of them still, unable still to understand how she had endured it, unable to understand how the boy could spend his time except in making it up to her every minute of the day, "the trouble I had with you!"

She remembered getting up from that first one dissatisfied. How could she have let so many things slide or just stay the way they were when she came to Mr. Hardy's house? They made the upstairs over into rooms for the children. Mr. Hardy let her have every whim. He was glad, he said, to be able to give hers all the things that Virgie's children never had.

Mrs. Hardy went through the chests and half-heartedly made a pile of ragdolls and teething rings, baby slippers, a moth-eaten hairbrush, a gold-plated diaper pin, and found herself working up a quarrel against her children. They were so selfish. Hers no more than anybody else's, they were just all. As long as they were at home they simply took for granted you had nothing else to think about except them; once they were grown you weren't supposed to have any reason for living left at all. The way they were surprised if you came out once in a while with something that showed you weren't thinking only of them at the moment, that old as you were you might still have a few worries of your own, absolutely surprised.

She gathered her keepsakes into her apron and sat down on the side of the bed. She thought of her life, how little of it had been her own. Before she got half a start she simply bolted to seed.

After a while she went up to the attic. Mrs. Hardy pulled up a crate and sat down, and opening the big old packet trunk was like opening a door and watching herself, young and gay, walking down a long hall to meet her.

At the county fair they were alone together once for a change, with a neighbor woman in to look after the children. Mr. Hardy told her not to waste a minute worrying over them and she wasn't. She couldn't believe it was him; he was like a boy, shot the ducks and threw the baseballs at the bottles and wanted to ride her on the Ferris wheel. "The Ferris wheel, Mr. Hardy!" she declared—and you a man, she started to say, with four children—but he was the father of seven, and instead she said, "And us an old married couple." She won first prize in jellies and fourth in cakes and Mr. Hardy sold a bull for more money than she had ever seen in one lump sum. Mr. Hardy took a drink of whisky with a man, something she had never seen him do before or since. She didn't scold him but said she was glad he took it; my goodness, everybody had to do something a little different from the workaday run once in their life.

Mr. Hardy bought her this mantle. It wasn't Mexican, it was real Spanish, the man said, but that you could tell by looking. It was heavy like wool but soft and smooth as silk with lace around the edges and must have had every color in the rainbow, but all blended and soft, not gaudy. The minute he laid eyes on it, Mr. Hardy said, he knew she had to have it. He smoothed it across her shoulders and put the ends down through her hands on her hips, saying that was how the ladies in Spain wore theirs.

Of all the moments in her life that had been one of the happiest. Mr. Hardy practically made her blush the way he looked at her in front of all those people. He said when the other women saw hers on her that man would sell every mantle he had.

In the wagon that night riding home, she laid her head on Mr. Hardy's shoulder smelling the good smell of him and listening not so much to his words as to the gentle sound of his voice. He was saying he had known beforehand she would like that shawl. She felt it again while he rode silently for a while. Then he said he never forgot how crazy Virgie was over the one he had given her just like it. He hadn't seen another one and thought he never would. They buried Virgie in hers, as she asked to be. Smiling, he turned and told her that as if he expected it to make the shawl all the more precious to her.

While Clara washed the supper plates Mr. Hardy sat by the stove and chewed and spat in the ash box. He felt as if he had put in fifty years' work all over again today, but at the same time he felt good. Clara had not made the fuss he expected and the job was done before he thought it would be, wasn't nearly as bad as he had been dreading.

It was easier to believe he had lived in this house for fifty-six years. Today he had turned up whole pieces of his life like something he had lost and given up all hope of ever finding. Lately he noticed he was going kind of stale; now he would have a lot of new things to think about. Going to stay with the children didn't make him feel quite so bad any more.

Maybe he did have to sell his house—at least he had a good house to sell when the time came, with good things in it, well cared for. He never realized he owned so many fine things. There was nothing he need feel ashamed to have strangers see and handle and own. It was a feeling you couldn't get seeing the place day by day that came over him now. His mark was set on this spot; the work he had done was here for everybody to see. There were not a lot of things lying around half-finished. The man who bought this land would be lucky and would thank him for working it into such fine shape. A good neighbor for fifty years, he had never had any trouble with anybody, always minded his own business. People would miss him. They would point it out and say, "That's the old Hardy place," no matter how long the next man owned it.

Actually he had done twice as well as most men; it wasn't bragging of him to say it. For he had raised not one but two families here and raised them the best he knew how. He had done well by his first wife and what things he hadn't been able to give her before she died, he'd seen to it that his second wife got.

Without Clara, thought Mr. Hardy, he never could have done it.

Mr. Hardy collected the stray bits of tobacco in one cheek and squeezed them dry. He shot the wad into the ashes and ran his tongue around his mouth.

"You know," he began and paused, waiting for Clara to reach a stopping place in her thoughts. She had fallen into a way of not answering when he spoke. Her mind was so far away, forever thinking over some old party or the time she had the twins or some such thing. She didn't like to be interrupted in her thoughts and he could appreciate that himself. In a minute she would answer in a tone of voice that let him know she heard him the first time.

Mrs. Hardy stopped washing a teacup and dangled her hands in the dishwater, waiting for him to call her by name. Why couldn't he at least begin what little he had to say with, "Clara this, or Clara that," at least show he knew it was her he was speaking to, that he had something he really wanted *her* to hear, that it made some dif-

ference to him who listened. She stood remembering the
early days when time and again he had called her Virgie.
Oh, she couldn't count the times he had done that, and
each time was like a slap in the face.

"You know," he tried once again, and she wondered if
the fear of making that same mistake over and over had
brought him to call her by no name at all.

Today must have taken him right back. Reminded in a
thousand ways of Virgie who had died young, his own
years had peeled in layers off his mind. He could see the
two of them young and happy together, only to look up
and find her there, stooped and worn with years of work
and sickness, no teeth of her own, a thing that could never
have been young. "Look at yourself!" she felt like telling
him. "Do you think a young girl would look twice at you
now?"

From the corner of her eye she watched him inspect
the things she was putting aside. Was he afraid some of
it was Virgie's? Wasn't it little enough for fifty years? You
have yours; leave me to my own.

Mr. Hardy yawned loudly. He stretched and the effort
sounded down his body like the snapping of many strings.
Clara was tired and he decided to leave her be, when she
turned and asked, "What were you going to say?"

He couldn't recall. "Nothing," he said. "It wasn't important." He smiled to show that she wasn't to worry
herself, that she hadn't missed anything.

No, she supposed it wasn't. When had he ever had anything to tell her that he thought was important? She stood
waiting.

"It takes you back, a day like this," he said, "makes
you think. Brings back things you hadn't thought of for
years. For instance—"

238

He looked up and there was Clara, her fingers pressed white against her temples. "Oh, what's the use," she cried, "of thinking over things past and done with?"

She started to say something more, then turned back to her dishes. Mr. Hardy got up and quietly stole off to bed. At the door he scratched his pate and thought to ask which of them was it that was always thinking over things long ago done with, but decided not to.

She had to sit; her backbone was like spools on a string. She rocked her head in her hands and wondered would all this misery never end. She thought of Virgie, Safe in Heaven these fifty years, safe in Mr. Hardy's mind, forever young and pretty. Surely, she thought, shuffling a finger across her withered lips, surely when the Lord called you you didn't have to come as you were. What else could Hell be?